BLI1

by *r.*

The cover: In Memory of the stealthiest nighthawk ever to patrol. We miss you Kai Kai ♥

Edited by THE VERY, VERY BEST HAWK-EYED (or should that be hob-eyed?) BETA READERS: R, Cindy, Tammy, Yui, Lyda, Linda, and ED.

1

To R: Thank you for keeping me fed, and for foregoing onions on our dishes, and by the way: CHECKMATE.

Glossary

Confession: I've said this before but I tend to skip over glossaries in order to get to the good stuff on my lunch break. That said, there are instances when glossaries and dictionaries are immensely helpful (Kristen Ashley's *Golden Dynasty* I'm looking at you—I must have flipped to your dictionary fifty times) and you've asked me to do this so I'm finally, finally putting in a glossary with some useful terms and words you might want to reference in this book. (But feel free to skip right to Chapter 1 if you're on the clock and want to dig into some BOOK. *P.S. good luck at work today! May this story mini-transport you to a sweet place* ♥)

NA'RITH: *a particularly mischievous race that excels at the business of obtaining a variety of goods by questionable and occasionally nefarious means, i.e. pirating.*

Iechydmaw: *Race of people transported to planet of Vfayr for the purpose of terraforming it.*

Garthmaw: *Iechyd for* The Breaker.

Narwari: *frightfully strong species of land animal native to the planet Vfayr. When the Iechydmaw people were sent to terraform Vfayr, they managed to tame a few of the obstreperous creatures and found them quite useful for riding, carting, and plowing.*

Smarl: *a befanged Narwarian smile.*

***Note: non-dog people are driven crazy by this word. This is a (slang) term that, in real life, is used for Shiba Inus, Aussies, Dalmatians, Jack Russells and a couple other funny breeds that pull their lips back and show their teeth. Not a snarl, but a *smile with teeth.*

A real word among dog-lovers, yet every couple of months, Amazon warns me that this book has been reported for incorrect content, and why? *This word.*

Salk: *Iechyd for girl, woman, and the female gender of Narwari.*

Salkells: *Iechyd for boy, man, and the male counterpart of the Narwari.*

Crite: *an exclamation common in some galaxies used for emphasis, especially to express surprise, frustration, or even anger.*

Krit: *an expressive Iechyd word used in various phrases (or even alone: "The krit?") to convey shock, surprise, irritation, impatience, or simply for emphasis.*

Tevek: *an intensifier to give force or emphasis, or to express surprise or alarm or anger.*

Gentling: *to make a creature docile, preferably by gentle handling when possible. Gentling also refers to easing/encouraging a fledgling Gryfala to take bonding interest in a male.*

Moonringstraked: *marked with circular stripes.*

Moonring: *fetching, to the moon and back attractive.*

Dijjü: *features peculiar to the Iechydmaw male in rut. Refers to the two erectile organs located on the foresides of their cranium that are highly responsive to sexual stimulation.*

Pakkluks: *warm, rugged winter boots typically fashioned out of cured animal hides.*

Sticks: *Vfayrian measure of time.*

Laps around the sun: *Vfayrian equivalent to an Earthen year and a half.*

CHAPTER 1

BRESLIN

My heart gives a little pang as I step back from the trio of Narwari. It breaks me a little to part with them. It always does. After this many sales, after saying goodbye to so many four-hooved friends, I should be able to walk away without feeling the tug of attachment. But that's not how this works.

With *most* Narwari you reap what you sow when you train them: give them your heart and they'll give theirs to you in kind. Nothing throws their shoulders into the harness harder than a Narwari who wants to please you and thrives on praise. Narwari are strong beasts bred for pulling heavy carts over rough terrain on planets where motorized vehicles either aren't affordable or the terrain makes it too difficult to traverse by anything other than a nimble beast.

And these beasts in this group are nimble indeed. Wonderful animals. They work well together, they work hard—and just as important, they've learned the patience it takes to stand at a hitching post, taking advantage of the resting time before the long haul home.

I've just stopped them in front of such a post, therefore resting is exactly what they begin to do. But instead of wrapping their reins around the weathered wooden beam, I hand them off to the buyer standing an armspan from me. It's a small movement, a subtle action. However, there is no more sensitive a creature than a salk and I happen to have one in this group of Narwari.

Of course she's the one that notices something is different.

I swallow thickly when I see the worry lines form above her eyes. I stroke her nose and her nostrils quiver wide as she blows out a shaky, uncertain breath—and this is what sets off her two male teammates, or *salkells*. Arching their necks, side-eying her and glancing sharply at each other—they're beginning to show the first signs of being uneasy.

In this moment, the command to stand still and rest would give them an objective, and following an order would provide them the reassurance they're desperately seeking.

I don't give it. Neither do I give the command for them to follow me. It's no longer my place. I was only ever meant to be temporary, and I've given their reins over to their new owner. They aren't mine to command any more.

I pat the three of them, force myself to turn, and walk away.

The *salk* swings her head towards me and looses a questioning honk. She might have been a trying creature at the start, but by the end, we got on so well together I knew this moment was going to leave me feeling hollow-chested.

She came to me with the most nervous disposition, but helping her find her place on this team has given her the confidence to master most of her anxieties.

Now though, all her hard-won calm is eroding with her growing concern as I break our routine and... abandon them.

She honks again, a wordless sound that manages to convey her plaintive, worried question. By now, she equates me telling them to *Stay* with the promise that I'll return as soon as I'm able. The pattern in the routine keeps her steady. Just like when I tell them to follow me, they know they're about to work: they know what to expect. So when I utter neither of these commands, of course it's upsetting. Encountering the unknown is always a bit worrisome.

I come to a full stop, sighing. All three animals stare at me and, left to right, you can read their expressions clearly: the dark male is uneasy, his brother is confused, and this female is in an anxious state of disbelief. I wish I could explain to them that they're being sold, and that their new master is good. Varold's stable sports more than one Narwari from me and they're happy, hardworking beasts under his capable hands—he'll love this trio. And they'll love him.

In time, they'll see.

The salk squeals impatiently as if to say *Well what are you waiting for?* Call us *there* or get over *here!*

Her thigh muscles twitch as she fights her instinct to fall into step with me. She lifts one foot—

"Stay," Varold says softly, and her hoof drops to the ground as she makes herself stand tall.

She's obeying the command, just like we worked and worked on. She's obeying *his* command, and I'm so proud of her.

She squeals again and I hesitate. I'm compelled to offer comfort even though I know it's only temporary: I do have to leave them, and it's the nature of the business that the transition takes work and some time. And naturally, it's best achieved when the old trainer isn't an interference or hindrance in the process.

I must leave. I accept this, and I don't want to confuse them (more than they already are) by returning once when they call me—only to ignore them when they try the same thing a moment from now.

But I have to try to say goodbye.

Tuning out the shifting of my mount, Meesahrah, behind me, I pull the nervous salk close. She spreads her jaws wide—an action that always calls for instant caution when the subject is a Narwari—but she isn't trying to bite. She's gasping for breath, and that makes me feel worse. She's just scared.

I croon, "There's a good salk. You've been trying so hard, haven't you?"

Her short tail, with three quarters of its length being flesh wrapped tightly around bone and one quarter being stiff bristled hairs, bears wary watching as it whips back and forth unhappily. But she's only swatting at herself in her agitation. She makes a high-pitched, shrieking cry.

To the uninitiated, it sounds like she's in pain. But this is her voice and she's just trying to tell me how she feels in the only way she can. I stroke her cheek. "A little anxious aren't you sweetheart?"

Her vocalization turns to a reedy squeal, and she presses her flat-planed cheek deeper into my palm, her eyes worried, her ears curled so hard atop her head they're overlapping. She moos in my face.

"You're going to do fine," I say with a smile, ignoring her breath. It's awful, with almost an undercurrent of llarolla carcass gone rancid, but for the most part I've grown immune to it. They can burp in my face and I rarely gag anymore.

Her muscles stop straining against the harness and the cart rolls back several hand spans as she relaxes herself. I pat her neck. Varold steps closer and offers her a treat which she gobbles as if she's been starved. As if I didn't have to add a lengthener strap to her harness at the beginning of harvest because her stomach's gotten bigger than the cart's set was made for.

She's not pregnant: she's happy. You could say that, one treat at a time, she's grown very, *very* happy.

She moos and her ears twitch when Varold extols her virtues. He even starts stroking the bases of her pronged antlers, telling her what a fine creature she is. He's not wrong. I tap her neck crest. "There, see? You're doing well and you'll like Varold, won't you?" I soothe before I drop my hand. She gives a deep sigh.

I step back, relieved she's calmer. Unfortunately, her crying has set off my ride, Meesahrah—or maybe it's my *attention* paid to the other female—but Meesahrah begins high stepping and dancing in place as I attempt to mount up. I suffer her attitude as I win my seat, twitching the reins back and forth, making her work herself in place until she gets bored, loses interest in wreaking havoc, and relaxes some. She's really a lovely animal when she grows weary enough to quit being a nit brain.

Do you recall how I said that with most Narwari you reap what you sow? I sowed nothing but spoiled peevishness with this one. Precisely how I managed to do so still vexes me. There's always one little brat—or in her case, an overgrown one. At eighteen of this Garthmaw's handspans high, she dwarfs each member of the trio in height. Unlike the worried salk, this female of mine is not several-extra-treats-a-day happy; Meesahrah prefers to keep herself all muscle—and aggressive, deadly grace. Somehow it manages to be attractive. More than manages: she's exceedingly fetching—therefore, she's easy to sell when she feels like behaving and showing herself to her best advantage. Unfortunately with this one, her 'best' doesn't last longer than it takes the new owner to shut the gate behind her rump. On the occasions when she has deigned to stay long enough to see her new stall—the shine wears off quick, and it always ends in her ultimately deciding she doesn't like her new territory, her new treats or her new master for that matter, and I get a Comm to come collect her.

She's like a scratched copper coin and I keep getting her back in change.

Meesahrah bears what's called a starlight pattern; a dark green blanket of color, heavily dotted with bright, lunar-white spots and white splashes that streak up each one of her legs and muzzle. Loudly marked as she is, she's very fetching. But unless she catches a Gryfala's eye (they adore flashy colors no matter the attitude under the ears) I've given up trying to sell her. I'm tired of having to buy her back.

As for this trio, relief hits me like a Narwari's kick when Varold leans in to bump the salk's forehead with his. Instantly, she gives him a little knock back, finally looking reassured. Her teammates lower their heads once as I wave a final goodbye.

The salk turns her head to the side so that she can keep one eye watching me, but she allows herself to be plied with soft strokes and a sackfull of treats. Her two salkells are looking less and less forlorn as they realize their third is no longer crying and food is involved.

I cluck my tongue to signal to Meesahrah that it's time to take our leave.

I dearly despise this auction planet but it's worked as a decent enough meeting point, and this trip has also provided me time to visit an old friend.

We'd split off earlier; me to make my sale, and him to stalk sales with the hope that something shiny would catch his eye. Unfortunately, it's his nature to be attracted to dangerous treasures, and when I reach him again, it's to find I'm nearly too late to stop him from doing something asinine and insane.

He's standing, transfixed, in front of an auction ring holding some of the rarest females in the galaxy. Normally very, very well-guarded females.

"You're going to bid on a *Gryfala?* Are you mad?" I dismount abruptly, dropping to the ground hard. I pay for my impulsiveness in the form of an instant twinge in my back that nearly steals my breath. Stark proof that I'm getting too old for this move. Just as I'm getting too old to take part in any of Ekan's wild schemes. I suck air in through my teeth as I straighten.

Ekan gives me a knowing look. "Training Narwari is hard on a man. Why don't you retire?" His expression morphs to one of profound excitement. "You could travel with us."

I give him the stare his invitation deserves. "With or without the Gryfala you're going to buy?" Each one of these females will have a dozen hobs searching for her. 'Owners' with any wisdom should be fully prepared to be hunted down. "Whether you rightfully paid for her or not, they will kill you. I've seen a Rakhii light a Krortuvian on fire for *looking* at the Gryfala he served."

Ekan claps me on the back. "I wish I could have seen that."

"Ekan? If you buy one of these females today, you'll get your wish—it'll just be more up close and personal than you're prepared for," I finish on a mutter since he's already turned from me. He hears me just fine: he's simply choosing to ignore that I'm absolutely right. "It's been good knowing you."

"Likewise, Bres," he returns cheerfully.

I grunt at him and turn my attention to the females in the corral. One of them catches my eye straight off. It's a waste of effort to hide this fact from Ekan, but I try.

He nudges me. "Like that one?"

When I don't answer, his shoulder collides with mine again. He's going to keep doing it until I speak up. I glower at him a moment before I deliberately turn my attention to one of the other females. My eyes narrow. "Something's not right."

Ekan's entire manner turns sharp as he drops his playful mood for his deal-hunter mode. "Do tell."

I jerk my chin. "Look at that one: she's heavy with a litter."

"Gryfala lay eggs," he murmurs thoughtfully.

"Then I say she's no Gryfala. That doesn't look like eggswell to me."

"No wings or claws either," he adds. "I thought that was patchy, but I tapped it off as overzealous control methods on the part of the seller—harder for the princesses to fight their captors if they've been stripped of natural weapons." He scrutinizes them with a seriousness he rarely displays. "I also thought Gryfala were bigger."

"They are," I confirm. "And these look..." I picture the Gryfala I've encountered. They're beautiful, all of them, but they exude danger. "Softer."

"Oooh, I like soft. I want to pet one."

"These are *people,* not animals," I snap.

He smirks. "A bit of advice, friend: pets, people, aliens—*every* female likes to be pet."

Ekan springs up, landing agilely atop the corral wall. He proceeds to pace it with the skill of an aerialist. "Teveking hells. Counterfeit Gryfala? This is *fantastic:* they'll fetch a fortune at resale and there will be no repercussions."

"Get down, you fool. And *no repercussions?*" I interject as much skepticism in my tone as I'm capable of. "How do you figure?"

He doesn't heed me and his manner remains unworried. "Real Gryfala won't rain down hobs and Rakhii-fire on us for buying and selling *fake* Gryfala."

I turn to him. "That's your definition of 'fantastic?' Is fiery retribution the only reservation you have about buying women?"

"Reservation is too strong. Hesitation maybe—" He breaks off his words on a hiss.

My eyes snake to the auction pen, following his gaze to a female being dragged out by her mane.

"That's just bad form," Ekan says, shaking his head, looking as disturbed as I've ever seen him.

Fair enough. This little show's not setting with me well at all. "Let's set our backs to this place—"

"That gravid one is mine. I'm not leaving her." He drops into the corral.

"What?"

"Look at her prying at that door—she's almost got it."

Giving him a dead stare that he insists on ignoring, I stop closer to the fence and watch where he indicates with a jerk of his chin. While the other females are facing down the auction buyers, 'his' female is using her fellows as a living wall, blocking herself from view and hiding her escape plot. Without taking my eyes from her efforts, I shake my head at Ekan. "I worry about you. You thrive on trouble and trouble is going to bite you one of these days."

He scoffs. "Trouble? She's a wee female."

The auction does not allow bidders to climb in with the merchandise. Therefore, the auction staff is bestowing their attention to my Na'rith friend as he disregards the rules—so typical for a Na'rith—and they don't spy the half-hidden female's actions.

But we do. We watch as she desperately—and unsuccessfully—tries to tackle the second door latch. I grimace sadly. "Determined little thing. Some animals are like that. Too wild: you'll never be able to find a pen that will hold them."

"She's perfect," Ekan declares. "I want her."

I stare at him. "You want yourself a headache?"

"A *challenge* and no: she's going to work for me."

I point to the female. "An imitation Gryfala she may be, but *that* right there is still no mild and meek-willed female who'll go along with any plot you try to connive. How do you figure you'll convince her to do anything for you, let alone do the sort of work you do?"

Ekan slants me a patient look. "Don't you know by now that I can talk anyone into doing anything I want?"

Meesahrah snorts in cosmically good timing.

And she's likely bored of standing in place—or maybe she simply dislikes my attention on anyone but her—but she dances her sharp hooves over my boot. I growl out the ingredients list of a famous Narwari skull and thighbone stew until she decides she's not so impatient to get going as she thought she was, and she stands so well you'd almost believe I owned a well-mannered Narwari instead of a tip-eared, hock-kneed, sharp toothed hellion with crooked antlers and a rotten spoiled streak.

I give her the look of distrust she deserves and for good measure send one to my friend too. "Ekan, I can't watch this. I'm headed back for your ship."

His chest crashes against the fence as he lunges half over it to catch my shoulder. "Don't you want to see what happens to your frightened little Gryfala and her..." he tilts his head and finishes with bemusement, "...whatever that creature is that she's clutching onto?"

He knows me far too well. Tossing a warning glare at my mount, I plant my boots, fold my arms across my chest, and settle in.

I want to be amused that none of the auction officials have grown brave enough to approach Ekan. They're so engrossed in keeping a wary eye on him that they don't spare a thought to the Gryfala *he's* avidly watching, and I have to respect my unbalanced friend. Nearly all the things he does are crazed, but very few of his actions are without purpose. And luck is with him—which is typical. A Na'rith has luck by the bucketfulls. And Ekan? Everything always seems to shake out in this Na'rith's favor.

That's a Na'rith for you in an urzashell.

Ekan and I observe the mock-Gryfala working the lock for another moment before I murmur, "Someone really better save her from herself."

Ekan's voice is serious when he says, "I know, Bres."

Someone bumps into Meesahrah and I reach past her to cuff the offender before she even lays her kick in. I pat her side reassuringly and to Ekan I add, "If that female gets caught, they'll flay her back until she wishes for death. And if she gets free among this crowd, she'll *wish* she was back in the safety of this pen where the worst she faced was a lash."

Without taking his eyes off the female, Ekan reaches over the rail and absently tickles Meesahrah's nose since she's sticking it in his face. I stare at her when she doesn't try to bite *him*. "Agreed, friend. Don't trouble yourself with thoughts of either; she won't be feeling the lash or be touched by the crowd." He hops back atop the fence, renewing everyone's attention on the brazen Na'rith that dares to disregard the rules. "Which one do you want?"

"Eh? I'm not contributing to the theft and sale of females, no."

He looks down on me—*literally*. "Oh come on. You're the only male here with those morals, and you know it won't save a single woman today—or you could save that one you've been watching and wanting."

"Wanting? I'm simply worried for her." I point to the way she's rocking. "She's under extreme stress."

"So is her hairy companion." Ekan cracks his knuckles like he does when he's readying himself for conniving someone into making him a particularly beneficial transaction—in other words, kritted filthy rich. "Have you noticed that the creature moves when she moves? Symbionts, you think?"

I roll my shoulders back. "Maybe."

"I hate to think what some of these males would do to them. The oddities tend to attract the wrong sort of attention sometimes. Take those Krortuvians over there for example. Ooh, don't look now, Bres; they're pooling their money together. You won't want to watch what happens."

I curse foully.

Ekan plays at being unconcerned, even adding an indifferent roll of his shoulders. "I can get us a good deal."

Reaching up, I slap my credit stick into his waiting hand. "Of that, my friend, I never question."

CHAPTER 2

BRESLIN

It's entertaining to watch a rogue Na'rith go to work. Normally they work their deals in packs, and that's an intricate dance and a dramatic show and a dirty war rolled into one.

A single Na'rith has to pull all the strings by himself, and orchestrate any tricks entirely on his own. Ekan is a skilled rogue though, and he doesn't disappoint either of us.

Where anyone else would be whipped for approaching the chattal, in true Na'rith fashion, he saunters right in and critically inspects what's left of the lot. "You're fetching *what* per auction and you don't even equip them with translators?" he tsks in disgust.

His statement is a scorching burst of flame over the dry wick of the fevered crowd.

Their grumble of agreement has the auction workers looking mighty nervous. The auctioneer looks like he wants to sew Ekan's lips shut, but only a fool with a death wish takes on a Na'rith—he wouldn't dare.

By the end of his performance, I think the only reason Ekan doesn't stroll out with the entire lot of females is because the crowd will revolt for sure. This way, the crowd's simply awed by his skill at managing to walk out with a fortune of two *plus* the hairy oddity.

All I have to say on the matter is the same thing I've said since I was a boy: I'm glad this pirate is on my side. Otherwise I'd be credit-less and still thanking him for whatever 'stupendous bargain' he set me up with; and I'd believe it was good for me. He's that talented.

Ekan moves to collect our females, but he does it at his own pace, blocking the lead-auctioneer from hurrying him along by slamming a hand against his chest, warning, "Don't TOUCH them. I wouldn't trust you not to bruise *fruit* let alone my new Gryfala."

The wild Na'rith coaxes the anxious female to stand and presses her into my keeping before fearlessly steering his swollen female out of the gate (not the one she nearly finished unlocking but the one in front) and strutting through the raging crowd.

I don't know how Ekan can stand to have the crowd pressing in on them—it's suffocating and I'm feeling massively uncomfortable.

However, the imitation Gryfala I've ahold of isn't tracking the crowd. In fact, her eyes don't shift their sight line. Bending down to peer into them, I see clouds in their depths. I've worked with blind animals, and in the little time I've had to watch this female, I've recognized enough similarities to be nearly certain that *she does not see.* At least, not the same way I do, not the same way the other females of her kind appear to.

Matter settled in my mind, I drop Meesahrah's reins because if she doesn't follow me by now, she never will, and Creator be with the next hapless fool who falls for her flashy, moonringstraked coat.

I bend, hook my arm behind the not-Gryfala's knees, and scoop her up. "I've got you." Thanks to Ekan's earlier announcement, I'm aware she has no translator, but even though she won't be able to understand me, I hope she can glean assurance from my tone.

Instead, she gasps and cries, "Myy dawwgh!" and various other unintelligible words that I gather to mean she's afraid that I intend to leave her companion behind.

My smile is grim. "No need to worry. You could say it's holding onto me." Her friend clamped their jaws around my leg the moment I reached for her. "Doesn't waste words, does it?"

I don't have to speak its language either to understand it's protecting her.

Thankfully, I was doing a little farrier work this morning before the sale, which means I'm wearing my chaps. The thick leather is enough of a barrier that I'm not yet pierced by the creature's teeth—though I most certainly feel them.

I tell the beast, "I'm not making her walk through this: I'll *teveking* take the bite. You'll have to deal with it, friend."

As the avaricious and curious crowd tries to swallow us, I release a growl louder than even her companion to encourage the crowd to—well, to stop crowding us.

I don't have her friend's language programmed in my translator so I certainly can't tell what it's saying, but I believe it's threatening the crowd right along with me when it snarls and latches harder onto my leg.

Ekan shouts, "Are you passing out engraved invitations to be robbed or are you going to join us?"

"Have my hands a little full," I tell him, "But I can still stomp you. Don't rush me." I glance over my shoulder and am fiercely pleased to see Meesahrah at my back, balefully eyeing everyone around us, baring her wicked upper fangs at them all. In a good snit, she squeals and half kicks her hind feet as she hops in place.

I take up her reins again, and press them into the female's hands since mine are full of *her.*

Confused, she accepts them, not holding tight, and that's fine—she's at least gripping them enough the reins won't drag on the ground for Meesahrah to trip on, or for some kritted waste-tube to snatch up and try leading her away.

When we catch up to Ekan and his own not-Gryfala, he shouts, "*Bres,*" before he tosses my credit stick into my full hands.

I manage to catch it, and am ready to level him with an unimpressed look in regards to his timing, when I notice that my credit stick isn't hot. Which means *it wasn't scanned.*

"What the krit," I call. "Why did you pay for my..." Guessing that the auction would prefer that the general populace isn't made aware of the fact that the Gryfala they're selling are counterfeit, I settle for simply referring to her as "...my female?"

Ekan moves so fluidly he could be dancing as he whirls, leading his mock-Gryfala at his side, walking backwards with her as he grins at me. "I wanted to buy your wedding present."

I'm leading an animal with more attitude than she has spots, I'm carrying a mock-Gryfala, and I'm dragging her mystery sidekick by my gnawed-upon leg. I nearly swerve us all off an embankment, such is my shock. "You bought me *what?*"

Delighted with my reaction, Ekan's grin grows even wider. He tips his head in my not-Gryfala's direction. "I bought you a bride."

And with that, he spins himself and his female around, and leads us onto the vehicle that all sky-farers are rightly wary to see: a Na'rith's pirate ship.

CHAPTER 3

BRESLIN

I'm known as the Garthmaw. My people, the Iechydmaw, first bestowed this title on my great grandfather, when he managed to break the wildness from some of the recently terraformed planet's native landbeasts, the Narwari.

As I mentioned, Narwari are large, woefully obstinate and wonderfully powerful creatures. I'm as demanding with them as my father taught me to be, and his father taught him. Narwari require a special form of tough love and learn the benefits of tameness and the value of structure through displays of brute strength. Sometimes my job demands that I slam sense into a few skulls and slap some respect out of a few hinds. But I'm not *incapable* of gentleness.

In fact, despite my outward appearance, and despite the harsh-seeming approach for my methods to achieving tameness, a great deal of my success with Narwari stems from my ability to handle them with care when they require it. Especially the nervous, frightened ones. *Not* ones like Meesahrah, who thrive on being misbehaving urchins, but the pleasant spirits who need patience and nurturing.

I hold the non-Gryfala female, our chests together, our hearts beating in time against one another. There were a few moments where she succumbed to extreme panic and fought me but it has mostly subsided. I soothe her with words she can't understand while she works to control her shaking and tears. At first she cringes from my touch, trembling harder when I drag her into my lap, her rump resting on my crossed legs as I fold her into an embrace she didn't ask for. One she doesn't want. I'm too strong for her to stop though. I take no satisfaction in her defeat. It doesn't take long before she's overwhelmed and in her frustrated helplessness, she sobs into me, her fists resting against my chest.

As difficult as this part of the process is to stomach, it's a necessary building block to *gentling* success. My care of her in these moments is what begins to build trust. I'm not her enemy; naturally she might chafe that I'm now her keeper, but here I am giving comfort when she's facing so many unknowns—her surroundings, her future, her 'buyer,'—me. Of course she's upset and frightened, but I'm offering her a sense of protection and safety, and it's a powerful thing. The part of her that's ruled by instinct is deeply grateful, and it's this part of her that forges the connection to me. She may even realize it's happening, but she can't stop it. Common sense is no match against the manipulation of instincts. It helps that I'm not preying on her need for comfort in some state of cold detachment; far from it—I'm opening myself to her just as deeply in return, because this stitching together of souls is necessary in order to establish a solid bond of trust.

The unavoidable danger of attachment is almost an unwelcome byproduct, but it can't be helped. Like the salk I had to say goodbye to this day, I can feel myself bonding to the helpless creature I have in my power; it's not ideal, not when I know the relationship will be temporary, but therein lies the tradeoff. In the case of this female, she needs protection; I have the strength—and no matter that she's an alien, this process results in the formation of a strong connection.

This situation *is* a little different though. This female is no animal, and I'm attracted to her: I can't help but notice that everything about her is unbelievably appealing. Even her scent is interesting to my senses; something floral and almost edible at the same time.

Her sobbing seems to be interfering with her breathing, and I shift my grip so that I can stroke her back. At first, just as expected, she flinches, but her system desires something—*any*thing—that can assuage her doubts and fears in this moment. It only takes two passes of my hand before she breaks and actually leans into my touch, absorbing comfort... even as she starts trembling harder.

This not-Gryfala's response is no different than a frightened animal, not really, and it makes my heart hurt for her. Halfway into this silent process we're undergoing, she bucks at the proverbial halter. She tries to pull away from me, her movements jerky and I can *see* her panic increase. In this moment, she's being attacked by fear and doubt: why is she allowing herself to be comforted by the enemy when she should be fighting to get free?

I could let her go, but I've tried this before with animals: it will have the exact opposite effect of calming her. To let her go now is to let her drown in these emotions; I can as good as wave any building trustbond between us goodbye—because what kind of partner lets their partner sink when they could save them?

"Whatever you're thinking," I tell her, "Be logical." I peer down at her, thinking logic is something she must be familiar with if she's anything like a Gryfala. They're uncannily cunning, and this female could almost pass for one. "I bet you could find a way off this ship, free yourself—but don't. If you manage to escape this ship you will not be safe." I press my luck by trying to pet her again—and Ekan's claim be kritted, she fights it this time and I grimace ruefully, empathy filling me as I imagine myself in her place. "It goes against the instincts, doesn't it? Of course you're compelled to try." I clamp her tighter to my chest.

"Noh!" she cries, and I whisper, "*Shhh.*"

Or, I *start* to. Her friend's fangs pierce through not my thick leg coverings this time, but my arm. Its great foreteeth sink into my skin, curdling my cordial reassurance into a curse: "*Shhh*—KRIT!"

The creature gives me a fearsome shake, worrying my limb in its grasp and as it does this its muzzle brushes against the fake-Gryfala—and the fake-Gryfala must realize what's just happened because she gives a hard twitch. "Kohtah!"

The creature lets go of me at once and bathes the side of the not-Gryfala's face with a frightfully long tongue. It's clearly a gesture of affection. I'm therefore unprepared when it makes a high pitched moan and lunges forward, hooking it's clawed paws around the fake Gryfala's delicate neck.

Shocked, I lurch to my feet, yanking the mock-Gryfala right up with me and holding her close. I check her over, running my fingers over her forehead, her short nose, her cheek, trying to see if any of her skin was snagged by the alien beast's short talons. Her skin is wet; from the creature's saliva and from her tears—though they've momentarily shut off. She's even stopped that heartbreaking hiccuping she'd been struggling to breathe through.

She's gone very, very still under my touch.

I've fallen still too: it's different touching her—very, very different than touching an animal.

After a moment, she catches my fingers. "Eyym fyyne," she says softly.

My eyes trace over her features. Nothing felt or seems amiss, and a glance down shows me her friend is staring up at us, anxious but no longer hyperaggressive.

Meesahrah wuffles a breath and lowers her head to examine the other four-footed being in the room. The small beast's dark hair stands straight up in response, making it look twice its true size and four times as fierce.

Meesahrah rears back and moos.

This causes the smaller beast to pull up short. Its tail, which had arched over its back aggressively as if it was preparing to lob a stinger with the end of it, slowly lowers until it rests between its hocks.

I peer down, trying to locate the stinger. Finding none, I'm relieved. I don't want it to hurt Meesahrah; she means no harm. She's simply curious—and who could blame her? It's not every day she encounters an alien.

I look down at the alien I'm holding.

"Kahn eyye tahch yoo bahk?" she asks.

Unsure of what she's asking, I direct my words to Meesahrah who is pawing at the floor and stamping in place. "Patience. I'll untack you soon, but you'll need to wait."

The mock-Gryfala's hand tentatively lifts up, and before I can process what she's doing, she places her fingers on my cheek.

CHAPTER 4

SANNA

My fingers land under his eye, on the sharp jut of his cheekbone. 'His' because the alien holding me is huge—HUGE. He has to be male. He's hard everywhere, from the wide slab of chest he's keeping me squeezed over, to the ribbed muscles of his warm stomach that's pressed to my lower belly, to the rock hard thighs that I was sitting on. His upper half is covered with only a thin, soft-materialed shirt, but his pants are made of some sort of rugged, supple covering with rivets that were digging into my skin when I was sitting on him. Guy clothes. He also smells good. Like tortilla chips fresh from the oven and pineapple rinds.

Another factor to add to my hypothesizing: he's carrying me like I weigh *nothing*.

My fingers ghost over his face, and when he doesn't move, not even to pull back, I touch him in earnest, trying to learn who—or rather *what*—I'm dealing with. His skin isn't wet or cold or gross. It's a bit abrasive, sort of like dragging your palm across freshly shaved stubble. It isn't unpleasant. The... surface of his face, I guess—it's pliable like skin—but weathered like leather, with deep grooves that interest my fingers because they don't feel soft enough to be wrinkles. Wrinkles roll, and move, and shift and this is not that. What else would the grooves be? Anything. They could be *anything*, he's *alien*—or so said the women I woke up in an *auction pen* with.

Kind of an incredible claim.

Per the evidence under my hands, I gotta believe them. But with no frame of reference, I'm struggling to understand what's under my fingers.

I wonder if I should stop. It occurs to me that these might be scars. He seems to be acting a little... I don't know, maybe nervous, though this might have less to do with the texture of his face and more like he's experiencing a bit of discomfort at having a stranger feel up his features.

To him, an *alien* stranger. When he touched me, at first I was scared. Then I was confused; my body was going all loose and relieved because the way he was touching me was confident but careful, taking charge of me but being kind about it—it was empathy in alien form. It sounds crazy, but that's absolutely how it felt. So even as my mind was screaming, *AH, AN ALIEN'S TOUCHING ME!* my body was like, *Whew, compassion: we can relax now.*

I wonder if his body and mind are going through a similar kind of struggle.

When my fingers trace the outsides of his eye sockets and venture in the direction of where tapered ends of brows ought to be, they bump instead against something jutting down from his temples, and he nearly drops me.

Just like that, I'm on my feet and he's holding my elbow to make sure I'm steady.

Okay... I try to pat him reassuringly, but he steps away.

Having him finally release me should be a relief, right? Like two minutes ago, I very desperately wanted him to let me go, and he wouldn't. But suddenly he's not touching me, and somehow... it's disconcerting.

Losing contact with him is actually making me *want* to call out for him.

I almost do—but that's when I hear the distinct sound of a belt whisking out from multiple loops and this light jingle of metal has me immediately tensing everywhere.

Is he going to *belt* me?

If he didn't want me to touch his face, he should have said something! Grabbed my hand, something! *Any*thing! I didn't know!

I'm braced, my heart's racing, I'm panicking like crazy inside—so it takes me a second to realize I'm hearing another belt buckle coming undone. And... another. How many belts is this cruel bastard wearing? By the fourth one, I only flinch a little. By the fifth one, I don't twitch and I'm totally confused. There's nothing coming at me, and by Kota's stillness beside me, I take it to mean nothing looks like it's about to harm us. So far.

A heavy thud tells me something just hit the ground. As long as it's not his pants—I'm good.

Something moves on what sounds like four feet. I sincerely hope it's just four. Six legs would creep me out. Anything more than six legs reaches the horror stage of my emotional state and I don't think I can handle more than terror, uncertainty, and disbelief right now. My emotional plate state feels plenty full.

By the sound of the thing walking, it reminds me of a horse—that would explain the leather leads that were briefly handed to me while I was being carried. And if it *is* an alien horse, there is a strong possibility that all the jingling and rustling belonged to this creature's gear being taken off and *not* the alienman's clothes.

I'm fervently hoping this is the case.

With much, much caution, I start to ease into a crouch, and when I don't feel the snap of lots of leather belts, I drop and hug the heck out of Kota's neck.

In true German shepherd fashion, she proceeds to tell me in great whining, yipping, yodel-groaning, growling detail about how she feels in regards to all these developments. I'm pretty sure she also launches into a retelling of events up until this point because she leans more heavily on me, almost knocking me over as she switches to an amped up conversational set of canine mumbles.

I thump her furry sides, hug her tighter, and finally, when that doesn't calm her down I take her cheeks between my hands, bump my nose to hers and tell her, "YOU'RE OKAY."

The alien snorts.

Kota and I both pull back and I feel her head turn in his direction.

"Is something funny?" I ask him, wondering if he can understand *me*.

Instead of answering, I hear his steps approach as he crunches over what smells and sounds like wood shavings.

Kota moves in front of me, blocking him.

He steps right past her, lowering himself to my level—I can tell this because his breath fans across my forehead.

I'm uncomfortably aware that I'm not wearing glasses. I never used to wear them, and for the most part, I still don't particularly care to—but they have their uses. Such as me needing to visit a store or restaurant that otherwise might stop me and demand proof (although they're not *supposed* to, some still do) that I'm really blind and not just sneaking in my pet.

Another handy use for dark shades? It helps shield where my stare falls. I sort of have an inability to know where I'm aiming it, a tendency that can make sighted people uncomfortable. More concerning: I've been told a direct stare can be seen as a challenge to both humans and animals and I don't want to find out how aliens take it.

Fingers gently wrap over my chin.

I tense.

Kota growls.

The alien's touch on me flinches and he grunts.

I can guess what's just happened. "Kota! No bite," I warn, but it comes out without the firmness that accompanies a normal command. She *never* bites—never—but she's scared and extremely confused and boy do I get why. A giant has carried off with me and now he's trying to take my face prisoner. She's got to be thinking, *This was NOT covered in training: time to improvise!* She has to know that normally I'd thank her. On Earth, if some guy carried off with me and caught my chin, heck yeah, I'd be all, GET HIM, KOTA, GET 'IM!

But we're not on Earth. This alien hasn't hurt me yet, and I'm hopeful that he's still wearing pants. This situation could be much worse. His grip on my face isn't hard or mean, and even though he just took a dogbite, the pressure of his fingers hasn't changed. He doesn't seem to be demanding anything, and it's the weirdest thing—with him touching me like this I feel like I could sit here all day.

Maybe aliens subdue through touch. That would explain the hugging thing he did to me.

It felt really nice.

He's an *alien,* but he held me, rubbed my back, encouraged me to cry it out on him—or so it seemed like—and here I am, leaning into his hold on my chin like he's a human-whisperer.

For all I know, he is.

Kota forces her way between us, her fur bristled stiff. It reminds me of the time I got to pet an African porcupine and its handler showed my tour group what it felt like when the quills rise up defensively. It was cool then. Not so much when your dog does it in response to an alien taking control of your head. "Poor Kota," I murmur as she crawls up on me like she hasn't since she was a puppy, causing my neck to stretch thanks to the grip that still holds my chin hostage.

With a dry huff, the alien releases my face from captivity.

"Thanks," I tell him, and despite her harness digging into my chest, I hug Kota to me until she calms down.

CHAPTER 5

BRESLIN

Meesahrah's head rises over my shoulder as she stares down—just as I am—at the pair of aliens on the floor clutching each other.

I'm contemplating what action to take next when Ekan Comms me. "Ready for you in Medbay," he says jocosely, and behind his voice his not-Gryfala can be heard still speaking alien. This means he hasn't yet fitted her with a translator, but this also means my mock-Gryfala still understands one of her own kind just fine, and whatever Ekan's female is saying to him has this female sitting up ramrod stiff.

I move to pick her up.

Mere moments ago, she'd spoken to her companion in a way that I thought meant she might be ordering it not to bite me. But as my arms encircle the mock-Gryfala, her companion looks me right in the eye, and clear as if we could communicate mind-to-mind, I read its thoughts: *What she can't see won't hurt her—but it can hurt* you.

It sinks its teeth into my arm.

Meesahrah gives an impressed cough. I curse.

The imitation Gryfala feels around for her companion's head, follows to where the gaping jaws are fitted around my limb, and she emits a sharp, horrified, "Kohtah!"

The creature hunches, triangular ears flattening. Penitently, it opens its mouth, and almost comically spits my arm out.

I check the saliva-covered area over with a gimlet eye. Thankfully, the not-Gryfala halted the beast before it could snap through my limb but by Creator, it's tried its kritted level best.

30

"Soh sahree," the mock-Gryfala says, patting my hand apologetically.

Her companion expresses no such regret, and in fact its eyes strongly assure me that if I attempt to reach for the imitation Gryfala again, I do it at risk of my limb and life.

I narrow my eyes, trying to discern what species this creature even belongs to. It isn't recognizable. It's colored in a warning pattern—dark black highlighted with gold around the danger areas: feet that end in claws, ears that cut sharply in the direction of my every movement, eyes that *dare* me to escalate our confrontation, and ambered yellow streaks that would call to mind late sunshine if they didn't bracket a long black muzzle full of teeth. Instead of having silky soft skin like the not-Gryfala, it has glossy black, stiff-looking hairs. It's *covered* in hairs.

Mistrust is clear in its gaze, which is extra expressive with the addition of alert golden brows painted above its eyes.

Despite the warning in its posture, it doesn't growl as I approach the mock-Gryfala it's blocking me from, and I hear the imitation Gryfala whispering alien words to it that sound placating in tone.

I squat down next to them. "We're hoping we have a solution for the language problem. May I carry you to the Medbay to be fitted for a translator?"

After only a few tense moments in which the haired alien does its best to glare a hole into the side of my skull, the not-Gryfala reaches out, bumping into my arm before taking careful, hesitant hold of me. I give her fingers a squeeze.

She exhales a small breath that sounds like a relieved one.

Her companion swallows a rumbling sound of disapproval, or warning—perhaps both.

"See? We're figuring it out, aren't we?" I tell the not-Gryfala with a smile before I move in and pick her up.

I'm pleased that her friend doesn't grab me this time, but the pleasure lasts only as long as it takes to arrive at Medbay. The moment the translator gun is pressed to the mock-Gryfala's ear, her companion takes hold of my thigh with violent ferocity.

"Crite, that looks like it hurts," Ekan says distractedly as he shoots the implant into the not-Gryfala.

"It does," I confirm through gritted teeth.

"I've never seen anything like it. Wonder what it's called."

"Don't know, but if it crushes me one handspan higher it'll earn the title of Destroyer of Future Offspring. Hurry up."

Ekan grins, pulling the gun back and loading another translator chip into the nozzle, "Gladdened to hear it hasn't earned that title—yet. Keep it busy for this part, all right?" and he aims and fires on the creature that's embedded in my leg.

The hairy beast's teeth abruptly tear out of my skin as it whirls on him, and Ekan *isn't* wearing chaps. He winces and braces to take the bite.

Before it can reach him, I catch it by the odd harness rig it's got fitted to its shoulders, and for the first time, I get a chance to really *look* at it.

I glance at the mock-Gryfala then back to the harness. Is this contraption for riding? The creature isn't very tall but maybe it's tall enough for her, and—I flex my arm and the animal slides towards me by only a handspan before it leaps forward with a powerful lunge—it's impressively strong.

The hairy creature's translator doesn't alter its vocalizations into understandable words, but the creature proves it has no end to what it has to say to us as it expresses its opinion loudly in spit-frothed snarls.

"Kota," the not-Gryfala calls, rubbing at the implant spot behind her ear. "I think it's okay. Come here."

The animal I'm holding immediately turns from its rant on Ekan, proving that it's well trained. I let it go. "Can you understand us, female?" I ask the mock-Gryfala.

She swallows hard, but she looks much calmer. "Yes."

"I consider this a kritted success," Ekan declares, and his female, who had been inching her way towards mine, startles when he grabs her arm. "Now we've got a job to do. Quest luck, as the hobs say." He pauses. "Or is that Rakhii? Tevek, if we had one of those..."

"Goodbye," I tell him, shaking my head at his grin. It spells he's up to no good. His female has no idea what she's in for with him, but she'll never be bored.

As if to prove this, he slaps his female's rumpcheek. "After you, my beautiful slave-bride."

His female snatches up his slapping hand—and bites him.

Ekan stares down at her in shocked silence. Then he guffaws. "Have fun with your new wife!" he calls over his shoulder, and my not-Gryfala goes stiff.

I start to reach for her, but think to warn her first. "I'm going to take you to the place we'll be staying on this ship." Carefully, I begin to lift her, and her friend gives an aggravated huff as if it can't believe my audacity. Or my stupidity. Before it can latch onto me again though, the not-Gryfala warns, "Enough, Kota. Follow us."

Kota's jaws close on the air with a snap and my skin tightens in reaction.

"Thanks," I breathe to the not-Gryfala, and she laughs. It's a small thing, but it has me staring down at her until her brow creases.

"Is something wrong?"

"No," I say quickly, "And you've done well shoring yourself up; you're calmer." I begin walking, relieved when her friend falls into step with me—no teeth involved.

"Thank you, I think. And I'll try to stay calm. It'll be safer for you," she says, sardonic.

"For me?"

"If I panic, *she* panics." She tips her head towards her friend. The movement must bother the not-Gryfala's injection site because she grimaces and presses her fingers behind her ear.

I wince. "Sorry it pained you. It was necessary."

She graces me with a rueful smile. "I figured that out when the two of you weren't speaking alien anymore. Thanks for that."

I grin. "Oh, we're still speaking 'alien.' And now, so are you."

Her lips tip up slowly as if she's weighing this new development. "I guess I always wanted to learn another language."

I roll my shoulders. "Ha! Wish granted. Many times over because I believe Ekan said you've got access to something like fifty planet's worth of languages and dialects."

"I'm not sure what the etiquette is for this situation, but I think I should thank you for shooting me then?"

I laugh, she laughs, and as we enter the Livestock area again, Meesahrah smarls. It's an unsettling snarling smile, and it gives me pause. I wonder exactly why and what she's so happy about all of a sudden. Not taking my eyes off of my animal, I set the not-Gryfala on her feet and hold her shoulder until she's gained her balance.

My staring draws Meesahrah's attention. Her almond-shaped eyes shift their gaze to me, but because I say nothing and give no command, her stare goes right back to the not-Gryfala. Or her companion.

Creator, I hope Meesahrah doesn't try to eat either of them. I do need new footwear this winter but no matter what I've said to her in passing threat, she makes a much better cart animal and mount than she would winter pakkluks.

Softly, the counterfeit Gryfala asks, "What's going to happen to us?"

I consider her a moment before admitting, "With a Na'rith—but especially Ekan—you can assume that he has plans for his purchase. Unless his plans interfere directly with you or—Creator forbid—*involve* you, it's best not to concern yourself."

When this only seems to unsettle her, I assure her, "He won't let his not-Gryfala come to harm."

"Not-Gryfala?" she repeats with a tinge of amusement.

"You appear remarkably similar to a race of beings."

She raises a finger. "How do you know we aren't the same race? Where are they from? Is it from Earth?"

"Are your kind naturally born with wings?"

She blinks. "Okay, so you might be onto something. We might *not* be exactly the same."

At this, I snort.

She relaxes by a few degrees and lets out a breath. "You tell me I shouldn't concern myself with your friend's plans. But what are *your* plans?" Her brows pinch, and she seems to gather courage to rush out her words. "I heard him make that little reference about me being your slave wife..."

I gently tug her so that she's fully facing me, both her hands grasped in one of mine. "I doubt you feel much like becoming a slave or a wife to a complete stranger."

She doesn't raise her eyes to mine, but one of her brows slowly inches high on her head. "It wasn't what I woke up intending to do today, not really."

Surprised that she can make light of her situation, I chuckle softly. "I'd imagine that's not often in your daily itinerary."

"Right?" Her hands are no longer cold as ice. I take this as a sign she's feeling an increment less stressed. Her breezy words seem to confirm it. "I only pencil stuff like this on *Mon*days."

I grin. "And what day is it today?"

She lifts her shoulders up to her ears, but she doesn't roll them back—she just drops them straight down again.

I stare at her thinking, *How alien.*

"I don't know." She puts a hand up to her forehead, her fingers poised like she can extract the memories if she only concentrates hard enough. Almost in frustration though, she drags her fingers through her mane. "Kota's wearing her harness which means she was working for me, so we were taken some time during the day, but *what* day? How long did we travel through space? All I remember is waking up in that pen."

I cast around for something else to say. I don't want her to dwell on what can't be altered. If possible, I want to see her happy despite her circumstances. "It's probably for the best. Especially if you were regularly penciling in marriage on this itinerary of yours. I can say with some authority that I don't think your Kota approves of you acquiring husbands. Krit but she has sharp teeth! Your harem of Monday-married males must be few in number and have no legs."

She grins before she breaks into full laughter, and it's like merry bells; clear notes stroke my ears before she tries to speak. "Try *nonexistent* harem! Sorry about your legs."

"They'll grow back."

She loses her smile. "Seriously?"

"No. I'm joshing you."

"Oh!" Her voice sounds a bit high, and a little bit weak. "Today I was given to an alien to be his bride, so you just never know." Her lips quirk, and although she's delivered this without lifting her gaze to mine, I feel connected to her with her stare fixed warmly on my chest.

I brush her ridiculously soft elbow with my thumb. "I wasn't intending to buy a slave, or a wife, let alone be gifted one. This is wildly unprecedented territory for me," I offer. "Could we pretend that we are alien to each other, and circumstances allowed us to meet by happenstance?"

The side of her mouth curls up even higher, which I take as a positive sign.

She confirms it. "I'll be so good at pretending that. You just watch."

I tsk. "One of us has to."

Her mouth opens slightly before she bursts with shocked laughter. "You didn't just say that!"

Pleased with myself for making her happier, I squeeze her hands again and let her have them back. "I did. And I'm glad you laughed; I was only teasing and meant no insult. I'm Breslin. Who are you, and where do you and Kota hail from?"

Much to my dismay, her face loses all traces of easy levity. "We're from Earth. I'm really hoping you might recognize the sound of it. It's a blue planet in a solar system of nine—well, eight, depending on who's theory the world is following—"

"Ah," I nod.

Her voice fills with hope. "Sounds familiar?"

My heart plummets for her. "I apologize: I said 'ah' to indicate I heard, not because I recognized it."

"Oh," she says, her mood changing like a lit wick doused by ice water.

To my great relief though, she doesn't retreat into herself. She offers, "My name is Sanna. I'm a human. As you know, my dog's name is Kota."

"Kota is your dog," I say slowly. "Is a dog a pet?"

Her smile comes quickly now. "Yes, and more—Kota is my eyes."

"Symbiont," I murmur and move my gaze to Kota who stares back, and the gleam of intelligence is plain to see. She's *Sanna's eyes.* "Ekan wondered."

"Symbiont?" She chuckles. "No one's ever called it that before."

"I've heard rumors of great tribes that use symbionts," I say thoughtfully. "I'd never met a set." I wave to Sanna through Kota's sight.

After a moment, Kota grudgingly sits and raises her paw in return.

"It's nice to meet you, Sanna," I say into Kota's gaze.

Sanna blinks and moves her head to the side, following my voice which is pointed at Kota. "Uh... Nice... to meet you too—are you talking to Kota?"

"I'm talking to your eyes," I tell her.

Sanna peals with laughter, and Kota tips her head, her lips lifting up in a smile.

CHAPTER 6

BRESLIN

"She uses her eyes to guide me—I rely on her reactions to the world to navigate mine. I can't actually *see* out of Kota," Sanna explains in a shaky voice as she wipes tears of mirth from her face. "Ahhh, thanks. I needed that." She sniffs and uses her wrist to mop at her eyes once more. "So Breslin. You seem like a nice alien—"

"Thank you. I've received the same impression of you." I walk to a small trough and press my thumb over the livestock tonguepresser, a mechanism that provides the leverage needed to open the inner valve; water trickles out and fills the basin. It sits low enough Kota will be able to reach it. I wonder if Sanna drinks and eats through Kota. Or perhaps it works vice versa.

Aliens. I roll my shoulders back. *You never know.*

Sanna's gaze is fixed low, but not, I don't think, for the sole purpose of listening to the water. She bites her lips but the ends quirk higher. "Right. What, ah, sort of alien are *you?*"

I kick the lever of a quad-leg seat to release it from the lock it had on the floor and drag it in her direction. "If Kota can't show you, and your eyes don't show you, then me telling you isn't going to be of much help is it?" Once I have the seat where I want it, I kick the lever back into the lock position and the sound of the suction gripping the floor has Kota sharply cocking her head, her teeth catching on her tongue.

I glance at Sanna to see her head cocked in the opposite direction with her lips slightly parted as she concentrates on the sound too, and I'm charmed beyond words. I sit down facing her, giving her space but staying within reaching distance. I close my eyes and imagine a blackout world. I hear everything, but it's difficult to perceive the space around me.

So much would be unknown: especially my 'alien' host. I clear my throat. "Earlier, you started to feel out my features. Would you like to learn me by feel?"

Her hand tightens its grip on the handle of Kota's harness rig, and I wonder if she'll decline. But then one of her brows rises as if I've issued a challenge—and when she takes a step forward it's a little hesitant, but it's not afraid. She holds out her hand. Kota, who had moved with her like an extension, watches us raptly.

I gently close my fingers around Sanna's small ones. "Avoid either side of my forehead but the rest of me is free for touching, so don't be frightened. In fact, there's no need for alarm—I'm a lot like you. Two arms, two legs, eight eyes—"

She nearly jerks from my hold, and I double over at the expression on her face.

Her lips purse in mock disapproval—but I see the edges of her lips trying to twitch up. "Did you just... are you 'joshing me' again?"

"I was," I confirm, "but bah! I could have eight eyes." I grin down at her and tweak the tip of her ear. "It's not as if you'd be able to tell."

The back of her hand lightly connects against mine and I guffaw. Kota makes a noise that distinctly sounds like a warning—until Sanna joins me in laughing.

I compose myself. "There, there. I'm done having a go at you—"

Sanna blinks.

"—and you can have a feel of me now." I lean down far enough that she can reach.

Instead, she surprises me by softly catching my hand between both of hers and she goes about examining my fingers, my nails, my wrist, my thick silver cuff. To signal when she's ready for more, she raises our hands a fraction, almost a friendly challenge in the gesture.

Still smiling, I set her hand on the bridge of my nose.

Her fingers stay well away from my temple *dijjü,* but the bases of them end at the corners of my eyes, and although I don't feel any special sensation whenever *I've* touched them, they react very, very differently when Sanna's fingers run over the length of the left one.

My body jerks in shock just like when she'd brushed them earlier. I thought I'd be better prepared this go around, but I was mistaken. My voice is hoarse when I explain, "That ridge you feel belongs to my *dijjü,* which expands depending on the..." *On the activity I'm partaking.* "Depending on the way I'm feeling."

At my words, her fingers seek out my matching and formerly unfeeling *dijjü* ridge on the right side, and I feel answering heat zip over my loins.

I quickly raise my head high enough that she can't unwittingly fondle them further.

My breath evens by the time her fingertips sweep impersonally over my heavy brow, my deeply set eyes, my cheeks that are set sharply enough to rival a Narwari's, and now she expands her map of my face by including the line of rough nodes trailing down my jaw, and finally, she drags her thumb across the edge of my chin.

When her touch slides down the muscles of my throat, my breath stops. For some reason, I was under the misguided notion that it would be uncomfortable *for her* to touch me. I never gave it a thought of how *I* would feel under her hands.

Lesson learned; I'll be doing this to every new Narwari that's brought to me. Right now, I'd follow Sanna anywhere, and I don't even know her.

Kota whines.

"Sit," Sanna says.

I twitch, and her hands stop.

"What's wrong?" Sanna asks.

It takes two tries to clear my throat, and it still comes out sounding so rough I barely recognize myself. "If my hindquarters weren't already planted on this seat, I'd have dropped to sit the moment you asked."

"Ha," she says and her hands smooth over the expanse of my incredibly sensitive shoulders. Until this moment, I didn't know they *were* sensitive.

Her palms land on either side of my chest, no fear this time as she touches me, only blatant curiosity and trust.

It's the trust that does me in. Because very suddenly, this session is losing its innocence where I'm concerned.

I rush to my feet, startling her. "You've learned me—are you two ready to learn your surroundings?"

Startled at my abruptness, she nevertheless recovers quickly. "We'd really like that. Thank you."

I take four swift steps back, and for good measure, increase it to two more. "Good. Quite welcome, and please allow me to show you around."

CHAPTER 7

SANNA

When he'd let me take his hand to trace it, I'd gulped. It's so BIG compared to mine. One swipe and it'd be like getting pawed by a bear. His fingernails are thick and rounded though, so not like a bear. He's recognizably humanoid, with just a couple surface differences. And *bigger*. By a lot.

He's got a strong throat, and I knew the moment I'd started to span it that my fingers wouldn't get close to meeting.

And I could *lay* across his shoulders. He's massive. Impressive. Very rawr-sized. I was gifted as a slave-bride to an alien giant. The thought had started to make me smile—but then Breslin had jumped to his feet.

I hadn't even had a chance to check out his ears or the back of his head. "Do you have hair?"

Breslin's steps slow.

I'm not sure why he's not answering, but then his steps bring him to me again. "Here," he says and if I'm not mistaken, it sounds like caution in his voice as he bends down for me. "Feel."

And I wonder if I imagined the reluctance in his voice with this word because as soon as I reach up and put my fingers on him, he seems to ease into my touch.

Rows of bumps cover the back of his head from forehead to nape. They're short, and when I press on them, they respond like they're fleshy: flexible but fixed in place. The tops seem tapered, like they're small spikes.

I balance on my tip-toes, trying to reach more. I hold one between my thumb and finger. "Is this part of you?" I ask. "Or decoration?"

"Part of me," he answers, not offended in the least. "Your males have hair?"

"Yes. Unless they shave it. Or unless their genetics stop hair growth."

"Does the difference disturb you?"

"Believe it or not, your lack of head hair doesn't even *rank* on the scale of strangeness I've encountered today."

At this, he grunts.

I carefully bring my fingers along the sides of his head, seeking out ears. When I encounter a thing on each side that feels stem-like, I follow them, bumping into flared edges and I think, "Success!" until they crumple under my touch.

I don't move, absorbing the sensory input I'm getting and not sure if it's bothering him to touch them.

Slowly, they unfurl under my fingertips and they feel so soft compared to the rest of him, with rippled edges and a fluted pattern, that I think of flowers.

A giant alien with flowers for ears? Instantly, I'm fighting back ridiculous giggles.

I think he knows it because he hums—but he doesn't stand up, so I keep going. When my fingers graze the underside of the curves, hot breath hits my forehead as he shifts, and I freeze, only to feel pressure on my hands as he relaxes deeper into my touch. To keep his head from dropping, I automatically cup his jaw. The heft of it surprised me before, and I give in to the curiosity I wasn't brave enough to explore the first go-round: I slide my grip so that I'm cupping him just behind his chin, and I drag my thumb over his bottom lip.

It's silky-soft, but firm—and inexplicably, my inner thighs clench. My body is obviously confused on why we're touching a man's face.

On a typical day, I don't go around feeling people's faces. Truthfully, I haven't done this since my last relationship. It's far too intimate.

But this is an alien, and it's not every day I get the offer to learn what an alien looks like.

Holding him—*touching him*—like this, I sense a peculiar change. Which is odd, because he doesn't move, and neither do I. It's more of a silent arrival of energy, and it freezes me in place.

"Sanna?" Breslin asks, and the rumble of his voice shakes me all the way down to my core. I lift my thumb off his lip, and ease a step back.

"We're standing in a livestock stall," he says, the subject seemingly out of nowhere until, with a jolt, I remember his plan—one that only moments ago, I readily agreed to carry out—was to make me more familiar with our surroundings.

"That would, ah, explain the shavings I thought I felt under my shoes."

"Allow me to show you the rest."

That's all he says before he backs away from me.

Kota right at my side, we fall into step behind him as he leads us around the ship's bay. Our location makes me curious. "Why are we in a livestock stall on a spaceship?" I ask, hoping that Breslin doesn't think this is where Kota belongs. If he does, then fine—but I'll be right beside her, and he better think twice before trying to separate us.

"The Na'riths agreed to transport my livestock with me so that I could make a sale. Meesahrah is my mount and she pulls the wagon we'll ride in to reach my home—she stays here, so I stay here. I don't feel right leaving her alone for too long."

"That's neat," I say. "I'm the same way with Kota—and not just because we're trained to stay together. I'd be wherever she was welcome, even if it wasn't necessarily as comfortable for me."

"It's plenty comfortable here." After a beat, he adds, "I hope you'll find it to be anyway—I hadn't considered you wouldn't. The keeping of gift brides is too new to me."

"Maybe you should be taking notes."

There's a soft puff of air. "Did you just josh *me?*"

"How's it feel?" I say with a grin.

His laughter sounds like thunder.

I try to hold back a smirk. "On second thought, maybe this is a thing you don't want to get too used to, you know?"

"Have to agree. Especially if these brides come equipped with dogs. My skin may be nicely ventilated now, but how many tooth punctures are *too* many?"

I snicker.

A moment of quiet stretches between us in which I hear Kota's soft panting, my shoes and her paws ever so lightly crunching over shavings, and Breslin's heavier but still soft-sounding steps as he leads the way. He breaks the silence first. "Can I say that you seem to be handling this all very well?"

My smile feels a little bit brittle. "It's funny: just the other day, my sister was complaining that nothing interesting ever happens. But *I* wasn't complaining: I'm happy with my life exactly the way it is. Yet here I am."

"Was your sibling taken too?"

"I hope not," I nearly whisper. "I didn't hear her in the pen. If she'd seen me, she would have called out."

"How were you captured?"

"I don't remember. Like I said, I woke up crammed in a pen of strangers who told me we'd been abducted by aliens. I kept hoping it was some bad joke."

"I'm sorry it wasn't."

He sounds like he means it. "Thank you. And thank you for buying me. From the sounds of it, there were some not-so-good potential buyers."

"You heard right," he agrees. "If you hold out your hand, we've reached the corner. To give you an idea of the size of the bay, do you want to walk all the sides of it?"

"Sure. What else is there to do?"

"Sleep, but if you're not tired, we can walk."

"I think I'm too wound up to sleep." I nibble my lip. "Are you tired?"

"I slept plenty before we ever landed. I'm fine and will be fine. Kind of you to ask though."

"Sure thing," I murmur as he guides us along the wall.

"Beware walking around in here; the stalls jut out from the—" he cuts himself off. "Hmm, farmers like myself use directions based on the sun's horizon position over Vfayr—that's our planet... which is neither helpful in a spaceship nor with you, I'd imagine."

"Not too much," I smile in case he's looking at me so he knows that I get how hard it is to adapt directions and translate them to be blind-friendly. "Kota will make sure I don't run into anything. She's brilliant at it." I relax even more with him because he's essentially just told me that I'm allowed to walk freely in here. I'm not a prisoner. This is a huge, *huge* relief.

But if I'm not his prisoner, and if he doesn't intend to keep me as his gift—as his *bride*—what am I to him? "Breslin?"

His steps pause. "Hmm?"

"Will you take me home?"

Even Kota stops breathing, and I wonder if she's watching something on his face. His voice certainly holds regret. "I have no ship of my own—I can't take you back myself. But I will ask Ekan."

"Does Ekan know where Earth is?"

"I have every reason to believe he desperately wants to find out."

This news does not sit as comfortingly as it should. "And... why is that?"

There's a pause. "I... I don't wish to upset you. I have reason to believe they'll agree to return you. Let's leave it at that."

I stumble to a halt. Kota's nose taps my leg and I know she's checking me over to make sure I didn't hit anything. On autopilot, I scritch her shoulder to let her know I'm fine... but it's a lie. They'd *return me?* I've just been walloped with the most ridiculous sense of rejection. I feel like I've tripped over an electric fence. "Because I'm blind?"

Breslin's hand suddenly swallows both of mine. "Sanna! No." He sounds so appalled that I relax, and I quickly blink away the stupid sting in my eyes. He sighs, and it's a reluctant one. "That rather prized race that I mentioned? The one you resemble? You and your fellow humans sold for an unimaginable amount of money today because buyers were under a mistaken impression, believing you to belong to a rare species. If the Na'riths can find Earth, they'll have access to more of your kind, an abundance perhaps, and with what they'll make selling them, the loss of your buying price will not give them pause then. They'll be making the trip to your homeworld anyway and that will be your chance, when the collection of others makes their trip worthwhile."

He's absolutely right: this is upsetting news. I'm gaping at him—they'd let me go home when they go to abduct other innocent women? Wait—and they're great plan is to do *what?* "You're telling me they're going to sell humans as knock-offs?"

The voice that echoes off the walls is from the other male I met earlier, the one Breslin calls Ekan. "Knock-offs—I like it! So many lovely new words from lovely new aliens. We're going to make *so many credits.*" There's unbridled excitement in his voice, the same way someone would say *coffee refills are UNLIMITED.*

Breslin makes polite introductions and asks Ekan about the possibility of me being dropped off at home when the Na'riths make their stop to pillage Earth. Ekan isn't as excited about this plan as you'd hope a space pirate would be, and not at all for the reason I'd expect. "You want to return my gift," he says flatly, and it's not like I can feel him looking back and forth between us—I hear that expression a lot, and as a person who has no visual cues, I don't pick up on glances. But I sure can feel the expectation hanging in the air as Ekan waits for us to explain.

Breslin remains reasonable, as if he feels I'm a person deserving of basic rights and freedom and maybe not just a wedding gift/slave/bride. Yes, I'm really hung up on this part. Where I'm from, it's just not done. My best friend asked for the full set of Patricia Briggs' Alpha and Omega books in hardcover when she got married. *Books.* Not a groom. "She was taken from her home, Ekan. We can return her—"

Ekan's voice is pointed towards me. "Is this because you're blind?"

"Ekan!" For the first time, there's an edge to Breslin's voice. It's aggressive and angry and more than a little protective. I'm touched and relieved—and stupidly, my backbone stiffens.

Ekan sighs. "Don't glare at me like I'm being insensitive, Bres. It's a reasonable question and I meant no offense, mock-princess Sanna."

Mock princess Sanna?

He goes on. "I understand that your handicap would make it impossible for you to assimilate into Breslin's extremely boring life and truth be told I didn't think of that when I bought you for him. If he's fine with his gift being set free, I'm fine with it too. But if your home planet is in the galaxy I think it is, it's going to take us a bit to get there. I'll do it, but I have a couple of runs to make first. Would you like to ride with pirates as we appropriate merchandise from individuals who aren't aware they're parting with it, or would you rather sit on a farm bored straight out of your skull until we hunt for your Earth?"

"You have a farm?" I blurt even as my brain tries to imagine scenarios where individuals learn they've just had merchandise get appropriated by pirates. I could be wrong but I'm having trouble visualizing that it ends well. My return ride home is going to get blown all to hell before I ever have a chance to get there. In the event it doesn't though, is Ekan's woman going to be offered the chance to go home too? *Or just me?*

I hate being singled out and judged and found lacking. For anything—evidently even my suitableness as an alien farmer's bride.

"My homestead has been in the care of renowned Garthmaw's—"

My brain's brand new translation software peeps, *Trainer.* Like... an alien animal tamer?

"—For generations. I'm very lucky to live on such a fine farm," Breslin answers, and his pride in his family's legacy is obvious. "But... if you'd rather stay with Ekan, the Na'riths will welcome you with open arms."

"Sanna," Ekan says not unkindly, "I want you to know that we really will." The physical origin of his voice shifts slightly as he makes his address to Breslin. "Bres my friend, honestly, she's blind. No matter how nice your farm is, she can't do a damn thing there and she'll be teveking bored as hells. Sorry. As gifts go, this wasn't my best."

"Ekan," Breslin's voice is tight. *"Friend,* I don't want to come to blows with you, but if you continue to talk about Sanna like—"

"Like what?" Ekan doesn't sound offended, or angry or worried—just matter-of-fact. "Are we supposed to pretend she's... now *there's* a nice glare. Look at you, puffing all protective. Creator, you're turning as savage as your animals—this is why I wanted to get you a nice woman. Maybe we'll find the perfect one for you when we round up new ones. Tell you what: you can have first pick. Any one of the lot you want, my treat."

Maybe we'll find the perfect one. Not *me,* because being blind and all, I'll never be anyone's idea of perfect, will I?

I shake out my fists. I don't have many buttons. But people—or aliens, as it happens, *who knew I'd ever have the opportunity to find this out*—discussing what I'll feel and predicting how I won't manage, and judicially deciding that I'm incapable of doing something, that

I'm *handicapped...* it rubs steel right into my spine. This Ekan couldn't possibly know that, and from the way he's talking to his friend, either he likes to get punched in the face or he's oblivious—but I'm absolutely internally shouting that I can do anything I put my mind to.

Even stay on an alien's farm, or so claims my pride. The knee-jerk, lifetime-honed reaction to adapt, adjust, and overcome is *strong*. "I choose Breslin."

My declaration comes out just as Breslin starts to snarl something at Ekan. Instantly, both males fall silent.

Kota shifts, her breaths short as if she's very focused. I'm right with her. "Is that okay with you?"

"If you're sure..." Ekan says so dubiously, my spurred decision forms into an ironclad affirmative. I'm DOING this.

"Enough with you," Breslin hisses, "Enough!"

"It was nice meeting you, Sanna," Ekan says so cheerily, I wonder if he's a little crazy. Breslin sounds two seconds from flattening him.

"Uh, thanks," is the best response I can muster.

It's a few moments before the sounds of Ekan's footsteps fade away. Breslin speaks, and his voice only holds a little strain. "I'm sorry. He can be too—"

"It's fine," I say quickly, not wanting the, 'he speaks his mind, he doesn't mean anything by it,' or, the old, tired standard 'I'm sure you're used to everyone looking out for you.'

Oh boy am I ever.

But I choose to focus on the here and now, where I stand on a spaceship headed for an alien's farm. Where I stubbornly declared I wanted to go, even though his friend intended for me to be this alien's blind bed warmer when I get there.

Huh, my hands are shaking a little. I am on my way to getting *upset*. I bury them in Kota's fur and she makes a groan that starts off like *Someone hurt you: let me kick their ass!* and ends with, *Right after you're done massaging me.*

Breslin clears his throat, but it's a beat before he speaks. "I wouldn't want to offend you by comparing you to an animal, but I have a fair bit of experience with animals. Notsomuch humans," he adds, his voice light and to my ears, desperately reaching for playful.

"Imagine that," I quip. It's not his fault I have triggers when it comes to the perception that blindness equates to helplessness. It's not his fault they were triggered. I release the dregs of my irritation in a rattling sigh.

"Are you regretting your decision?" Breslin sounds like he's wincing.

Shavings crunch as he moves closer, but he doesn't crowd me. He's been incredibly conscientious so far. If I had to pick between him and his friend—and essentially, I just did—I'd still pick him. "Not yet."

Scuffing, like the sound the heel of a man's hand makes as he scuds it over his beard stubble, reaches my ears. Which is kind of peculiar since Breslin has no beard. Concentrating on this quandary almost makes me miss what he says next. "You can't get home at this moment, but that doesn't mean *never*, right?"

My throat tightens. "I really hope not." I squeeze the handle of Kota's harness. "Let me guess: you're advising I don't panic?" But just saying the word panic kind of makes me panic.

"That is precisely my advice. Why are you breathing so—I'm reaching for you," he informs me, and Kota doesn't growl as he takes careful hold of my wrist and tugs me close enough to pat my back until I calm down a little. "Shhh. It'll turn out well. Just settle in with me for now, and *don't* panic. I don't want you to be upset."

Despite myself, I choke on a watery laugh. "I'm glad my temporary owner is nice. Thank you."

"Don't..." he starts softly. "Please don't think of me as your owner. Just... consider me a friend."

CHAPTER 8

SANNA

Breslin leans close. "I'd like to introduce you to my motley crew."

I pull back a little. "The pirates?"

"No, my four-legged friend."

He laughs at whatever he sees in my expression. "You're afraid there are 'aliens' on four legs?" I can hear the smile in his voice. "She's more like your friend Kota, somewhat."

"So eight eyes, huh?"

Breslin's chuckle makes me smile even as I fake a haughty sniff. But seriously, I very strongly doubt that there's much similarity between his four-footed friend and Kota, but it seems rude to say that out loud. Instead, Kota and I follow him to be introduced to his mount, and the scent I've quickly come to associate as *Breslin* gets stronger. Dark, earthy, and somewhat 'wild'-scented for lack of a better word, I have an 'aha!' moment—this scent is actually Breslin's alien horse.

"This is Meesahrah."

Somehow, in these three words Breslin manages to infuse both affection as well as a frightfully large dose of warning.

Why he feels he has to add warning, and *who* exactly he's warning is the mystery, because I could be wrong, but I get the sense it's not intended for Kota and me.

"If you reach out with your right hand, she'll bump your fingers with her nose. Yes, like that."

Her nose is soft—*so* soft. Velvety-fine and it moves under my touch. I accidentally poke a finger into her nostril and she disappears. "Oops,

I'm so sorry!" I tell her. "I don't usually go around stuffing my fingers up anyone's nose. That was an accident."

"She's alright," Breslin chuckles. "It only surprised her. She's not shy; she'll rub them on you when she's got a booger."

"That's lovely of her!" I'm smiling and my lips stretch even further when her nose presses into me, shifting back and forth over my fingers like it's twitching with curiosity as she explores me.

"Her lips are directly under her nose, and they're very sensitive. She's like a youngling; she mouths everything she's curious about so don't be alarmed if she—"

Her lips close over my hand.

Despite myself, my first instinct is to jerk back. My hands are my eyes; for some blind individuals, our digits become highly attuned to the lightest pressure and texture. They develop or even overdevelop a super tactile sense.

"That's enough, Meesahrah. Let her go."

I'm about to breathe a sigh of relief—but instead of obeying the command, Meesahrah keeps on playing. Strong, thick lips inch up my wrist and my knuckles are sucked onto a bed of soft, spongy tongue as more of my hand disappears inside her mouth.

Edges of teeth rim next to my thumb and on the opposite side along my smallest finger. *Sharp* teeth. This just got serious.

"Meesahrah," Breslin warns. "Don't test me."

Hot breath fans on either side of my elbow as Meesahrah exhales—to my ears—quite petulantly.

Kota makes a warning noise—but she's drowned out by Breslin's strange popping snarl. He made the same odd sound when he was carrying me through the crowd of aliens. Boots thud and he forms a wall at my back and with my arm being a quarter of the way inside this animal, I can sense that he grabs ahold of perhaps her ear and it seems like he's speaking directly into it when he growls, "I won't tolerate you giving her attitude. You act like a lady with her or you'll be this fall's throw rug at the hearth, do you follow me you egg-headed slapperfish?"

She spits out my hand.

Biggest. Breath. Of relief. "Whew! Thanks..."

Breslin's still chastising his pet. "The only thing thicker than your hide is your skull. If you don't straighten up, I'll be using strips from your back for the next shock absorbers on the winter sleigh *do you follow me?*"

Meesahrah makes a weird mooing sound. Maybe it's apologetic. But it sounds put-out, like he's overreacting about the way she tastes his guest's hands.

Breslin shifts, the heat from his body impossible to ignore as he towers over me, and my guess is he's checking me over closely. "I sincerely apologize for her deplorable behavior. She's normally not so..."

"Hungry?" I tease.

Hearty laughter bursts against my forehead. "She doesn't normally go that far touching people. A bump with her snout to acknowledge them but no more. Here, let me have your hand."

"My hands must be super cute. You're not the first alien to want them today."

"Aren't you funny," he murmurs as he gently takes hold of my wrist and drags it across his very, very tightly muscled thigh.

This alien has really *very* nicely defined muscles.

My face feels suddenly very warm.

His fingers are big and solid and their light touch is making my insides start processes that they shouldn't be interested in starting, especially when he's doing so little. Confidently, he declares, "There. Dry."

I'm uncomfortably aware that *other* parts of me are quite suddenly decidedly less dry.

I clear my throat. "Um, what were you threatening her with? Shock absorbers?"

"Oh that," he grunts. He releases my wrist by carefully placing it against my side.

My body, for its part, remains limp and pliable for him, soaking up his concerned, gentle attention. I'm aware of him so suddenly and so strongly that it's distracting. I take a step back, and Kota moves right with me.

"This side of the galaxy has seen advancements of all kinds in technology, but the most affordable, reliable option for transportation on the planet I hail from is conveyed by recalcitrant beasts. The vehicles we use—wagons and sleighs—absorb the bumps and jostles of the road using a series of multi-layered leather straps. They take a beating like nothing else. Not unlike Meesahrah," he adds in a threatening growl that somehow holds affection.

"You use *sleighs?*" It sounds so old-world and quaint.

"Sleighs and wagons. I mentioned riding to the homestead—there's a wagon stored in the next bay. That's our way home."

Riding in a wagon. Somehow, that strikes me as being almost as incredible as riding in a spaceship.

"May I place my hand on your back?"

"Uhhh..."

"To guide you," he explains. "We can go up to the next level of the ship and walk around."

"Sure."

The heat of his palm sears low along my spine and I swear I feel my face heating up again. It's a ridiculous reaction; people touch me all the time. In fact, most don't even ask—good Samaritans see a blind person and the first thing they are compelled to do is reach out and grab them. Their hearts are in the right place, but to abruptly be latched onto without warning is a bit unnerving. Not to mention dangerous if we lose our balance when a stranger suddenly tows us along. That this alien so conscientiously gains permission first... well, it's really, really nice.

Just like the light pressure of his broad hand.

"In my early years, I used to build them," he says seemingly apropos of nothing until I recall that we were talking about wagons. "First day on the job, I was told to fetch a wiffletree coupling. I thought, 'What in the tevek...' By the time they ordered a thing called a lazyback iron, I thought they must be joshing me. Who named these parts? *Perch plate whip socket,* a *stake pocket.* It all sounded ridiculous to me."

"But you caught on and built beautiful wagons?"

"Wouldn't that make a nice story?" Humor coats his words. "I wish I could boast such a fine ending, but at best, my efforts were passably sufficient. No one would ever mistake me for having a gift in that area. I was as useless as a Narwari's front fangs are long."

Considering where my hand had been a few moments ago, this adage is just the littlest bit unsettling. It's probably a good thing he didn't share it until *after* his friend sucked my arm into her mouth.

CHAPTER 9

SANNA

Kota whines and I stroke my hand in the space between her ears. "I bet everything looks different, huh girl?"

We're sitting huddled under the canvas top of the first wagon Kota and I have ever had the experience of sitting in. Ekan helped Breslin roll the 'vehicle' out (it seems super strange to refer to it as a vehicle, but I suppose it is), but first they got us tucked safely inside while the pair of friends started in on their goodbyes.

It's POURING rain. It fit my mood a few minutes before, when the other human woman on this ship, Beth, gave me a desperate hug.

As hot drops landed on me—teardrops, not rain—I almost started crying too as we clutched at each other, two complete strangers far, far away from home—but then Ekan interrupted, exclaiming, "You'd think we were beating them! There's no need for tears. You're both in good hands—mine are better; sorry, Sanna—but you'll see each other again soon."

Since that (cocky) pronouncement, I've breathed a little easier.

Kota's head turns this way and that, and I know she's watching Breslin because whenever he speaks, her head is already pointing in his direction.

Finally, Ekan calls, "Bye for now, Sanna!"

"Bye for now," I answer back, holding him to this promise even though the idea of me being picked up again does not bring much relief. The idea that I get to go home while other women are going to be abducted isn't something I feel right about getting excited for.

The wagon dips low as Breslin hauls himself onto the bench beside Kota and me. "I'm sorry. I wish you could experience the beauty of my home without such miserable weather."

I send him a smile. "Every storm brings flowers, right? Take being abducted and sold to an alien, for example. I'd consider that a pretty big storm. So far, you're quite the cheery little—or very big—flower in all this."

His chuckle makes all my nerve endings sing. "No one's ever dared to call me a flower before."

I give him an exaggerated shrug. "It's not every day you're gifted a human slave-bride."

Now he outright laughs. "Said true, Sanna. Said true."

He clucks to Meesahrah and gives her the command to haul out.

Despite the excellent leather strap shock absorbers this wagon surely has, it's no smooth-riding BMW or Mercedes-Benz. We roll along for a few minutes in silence, though it's the very farthest thing from quiet: the sound of rain pounding against the canvas wagontop is deafening and even drowns out the grinding creaks of the wooden board and metal frame that I can *feel* groaning and creaking even if I can't hear them.

My teeth clack together hard when the wagon lurches. Kota and I are slung forward. We don't sail off the bench though—we're caught by a big, strong arm. *"Tevek!"*

"What's wrong?"

"We just got stuck," Breslin mutters darkly.

"Stuck how?" I ask.

"Wagon wheel in a kritted mud sinkhole—" A series of alien words that do not translate issue forth rapidly from my (up until this point) unflappable, amiable companion as he drops his arm from us and hops off the wagon. "I'm going to have to lift the entire frame to free the wheel. Hold on to the seat for balance, because there's going to be a jolt when Meesahrah hauls us out of the mud, understood?"

I grab onto the edge of our seat with a death grip. "Got it. Thanks."

"Good." A moment passes and the wagon shudders mightily—but we're not freed.

The shudder comes again and Breslin's grunt is a massive thing and speaks of excessive effort a millisecond before the world tilts, the whole wagon finally rising up on one side.

"Meesahrah," Breslin's voice is strained with effort, "please, walk on."

Nothing happens.

"*Meesahrah?* Walk. On."

...Still nothing.

Kota's tags jingle and her ear knocks my hand as she cocks her head.

Breslin's voice explodes. "THROW RUG!"

The wagon gives a half-hearted heave.

"*Good.* Hup, hup!"

Nothing *more* happens.

"TEVEKING,   SWAY-BACKED,   KRITTED, BUCK-TOOTHED—"

The insults would blister my ears with their intensity if I didn't find them oddly amusing. I bite my lips.

By the time Breslin reaches the end of his tirade, he's panting and back to being calm, which only makes it funnier when he delivers a conversational, "Your dam gave birth to you under a bad moon, didn't she?"

I'm silently snickering into my hands when the wagon sinks back into the mud and Breslin's voice appears at my ear. "Keep laughing, Sanna. You're going to drive."

I rear sideways, bumping into Kota. "Me? I don't know how—"

"You're about to learn."

Leather lines are draped over my lap. A rod pokes the webbing near my thumb. "Open your hand," Breslin says patiently. "This is the whip."

"I'm *blind* I don't think it's a good idea to be whipping at anything!"

"You won't be. Meesahrah's got her eye on it though and if she needs incentive, raise the whip up like you're about to pop it, and she'll move."

I worry my lip and grip the reins, feeling the stitches along either edge of the leather. Feeling them out, taking the time to learn them grounds me and the panic subsides a little.

The fight against the mud's suction is fearsome. I can feel the power it takes Breslin to haul the wagon up again—the slog we're stuck in seems to be sucking at us harder this time around.

"Sanna," he grunts, his voice strained and causing warm shivers to run up and down my body that have nothing to do with the mist of rain chilling my skin, "Lift that whip and direct her a little to your left."

I pull on the rein. But I'm not sure how hard to pull it. I feel at a large disadvantage not being able to *see* Meesahrah respond, but just as I lament this to myself, movement carries through the line and bells jingle, signaling she's turned a little. *I hope she knows what's enough...*

"Tell her to walk on," he instructs.

I try, but she doesn't respond to me at all. Dogs are like this—some dogs know you're not their owner, so they don't have to listen to you and that's that. "Bres—"

"Shout it," Breslin instructs.

"I can't—"

"Yes you can. SHOUT IT."

"Meesahrah, WALK... ON." For good measure, I weakly lift the whip.

The wagon jumps forward.

"GOOD SALKS!" Breslin whoops.

My translator pops, *Good girls!* into my head. And I can't tell if Na'rith technology is expressing the sense of praise in the words, or if

I'm reacting to what I hear in Breslin's voice, but warm approval washes over me, making my skin tingle.

It feels good—but it's not enough to calm my nerves. Not by a long shot. "What do I do now?" There may be a slight note of panic coating every word. I'm no longer pulling the rein left; I don't know how wide the road is, or if Meesahrah's corrected us to a straight line, I didn't hear the jingle of the harness but I might have missed it over the sound of the rain—

"Easy, whoaaah," Breslin says easily and just like that, Meesahrah slows us to a halt. "I should be grateful for the bath and shower, but I don't feel very clean," he comments as the wagon dips and he lands on the bench next to us again. A slightly broken up, muffled inhale leads me to imagine he's scrubbing his hands over his face and slicking water and mud off of himself. "You're doing well, Sanna. Let's have you drive us home."

It's ridiculous that an alien telling me I've done a good job should affect me at all, but a gratifying pulse zips through me at his words. "Thanks. And okay then; tell me what to do."

Breslin's instructions are all given in a patient, measured manner, and it makes me feel ridiculously accomplished to drive us along the rutted road, and feel Meesahrah respond to cues that I feed her through the reins and with my words.

Some time later, Breslin murmurs, "We've made it here. Now say, hup, hup, slowww, just like that."

With more confidence than I would have thought myself possible, I tell an alien creature (that tried to go full Dyson on my arm) to trust that I know what she should do—and she does, she *trusts* me and listens obediently. It's hugely... satisfying.

It's second only to clocking in at my job. I'm employed in a factory that makes body pillows and pet beds. I force Poly-fil baffles into impossible shapes and fight stuffed bolsters inside of their proper covers. It's not the work per se that I love; it's the independence. Getting to drive a vehicle for the first time in my life? This is *cool.*

Kota shifts beside me and makes a four-part, soft, whuff-whuff-whine that she does whenever we encounter something new and she's gearing up to meet the challenge.

I know how she feels.

"You did wonderfully," Breslin comments.

It's simple praise but it lights me up inside so that I feel like the sun is shining on me, heating me up and we're not about to have an ark float by, despite the current conditions.

"I'm going to hop down and open the barn, and you can direct her in while I close up the gates."

"How will I know where to go and when to stop her?"

"She will know. Don't give it any worry."

I give her the command to walk on when Breslin tells me to, and with no prompting from me, Meesahrah gets us rolled to the right place and slows to a stop on her own.

Her harness jingles and the lines abruptly slap in my hands, making me tighten my grip on them.

"Stop it," Breslin warns from farther away than I'm comfortable with considering I can't see what our ride is doing.

Meesahrah moos but the jingling falls silent and the reins relax.

A moment later, Breslin is at the side of the wagon. "Will Kota need to relieve herself? Does she do this outside like an animal or..."

"Yes, like an animal," I confirm. "Where should I walk her?"

"Allow me to help you down," he says and his hand is rough in mine and dripping water.

I've secretly been dreading the getting-down part. It's a bit daunting because when I was on the ground, I found out the step to get *up* here is near my shoulders in height and there's only the one. To get me seated, Breslin lifted me up and set me in and I wonder if I'm exiting this way too. It's a long, long jump down to the ground otherwise.

"Put your hands on my shoulders," he instructs.

The fabric of his shirt is soaking wet but his shoulders are pleasantly warm and deliciously hard. Instantly, I'm warm all over despite the chill.

His rough hands close around my waist and he picks me up by my hips and sets me on the ground.

I'm still recovering from his help when his attention turns to my best friend. "Kota, can you make it or should I pick you up?"

Kota leaps down effortlessly behind me.

"What a bright salk. Alright, Sanna, I'm taking you by the elbow," he warns as he moves his touch, "And if you want to stay dry you can walk her the length of the barn if you think she'll go in the shavings, or we can go through the side door if she needs to go outside."

"Unfortunately, probably outside. She's never been allowed to go to the bathroom in any sort of building and she isn't likely to start now." Some people who've never had a dog don't think they can feel shame, but Kota does. Maybe it's a German shepherd thing, but they don't even like to get sick on the carpet. It bothers her when she does things she knows aren't proper.

"Outside it is then. Sorry, Meesahrah, you stay."

Bells jingle.

"I said *stay*—I'll be back soon."

There's a loud huff and the bells fall silent.

Breslin mumbles, "I'm going to be making that up to her until she stops pouting."

"Why is she pouting? Is it the rain?"

He snorts. "No, she doesn't mind the rain. She just doesn't like to share my attention. If she followed us out she'd feel better spoiled, but until she's unhitched, she's just going to have to wait."

My tongue presses the inside of my cheek, and I feel my lip twitch. "Ah. I see. Kota gets that way a bit. I don't think she's quite on par with Meesahrah though. She sounds pretty..."

"She is. It's her only charm."

"...high maintenance."

"Oh you have no idea."

I find myself grinning at his tone. It's that of a longsuffering owner—one undeniably fond of his brat.

Before we make it out the door, Breslin stops us and I hear a light rustling. "Here, I happen to have a slicker for this weather. If only I'd packed it in the wagon," Breslin says wryly. "Though that wouldn't have saved me from the knees down. I found out I have a hole in my boot the moment it filled up with cold slime."

"Aww," I grimace in commiseration. "Sorry..."

"It's fine. Take the slicker: it'll make for a dryer walk for you."

"Thank you." I move to take it but end up standing still when he seems to want to help me into it. I don't get the sense he thinks I'm helpless. It seems more like a polite, otherworldly etiquette thing. Although, I think my parents do this. I can see why. It's... really nice.

But it's a weird walk. If I'd woken up right here, I'd have known I was in a very strange place and far from home. The air is so crisp and clean, I feel both more awake and more relaxed. There's no car horns, no chatter of a crowded sidewalk, no buzzing of electric lightposts along the street, no water running off the the street drains. The only sound is the softly-falling rain.

That and the single squelching step for every other step Breslin takes. Imagining the mud oozing through the hole in his boot, my smile is all sympathy. "Are you the only one that lives in this area?"

"The closest neighbor is three sticks away. His Narwari are due for a hoof trim and he's got a young bunch that he wants trained to harness, so you'll get to meet him if you like."

"I... I'm not sure I should make connections. I'm just going to have to leave them." Rainwater splashes over my shoes, which were once very new, very lovely tennis shoes that felt so light it was like walking on clouds. They now feel like squishy lead weights.

Breslin's growl somehow conveys the sense that he's hearing what I'm saying, a quality I appreciate. "Understood. But Ekan was right: you'll go mad if you stay inside all day. My house is nothing more than a place to get out of the weather and rest when the work's done."

I feel my cheek dimple as I hold back a smile. "But it's a farm. Is the work ever done?"

"No it is not. Therefore, it's a kritted small house."

Kota finishes her business and we head back to the barn with Breslin saying, "I need to untack Meesahra and get her settled for the night."

"Can I help? Or if there's nothing I can do, tell us where to stand."

"Right here," he directs me with a hand lightly guiding me at my back again. "You can pace straight ahead if you feel the need to stretch your legs some more. This will take a bit. I need to check Meesahrah's hooves for stones and packed mud."

"That's fine," I assure him. His actions have shown him to be a considerate owner, and I admire him for it. Since he essentially owns me just as much as he does Meesahrah, it's also reassuring.

Breslin hums a little as he unstraps pieces of gear from off of our ride. When the sound of bells and buckles stop ringing, he addresses his animal. "Give me your hoof."

Then: "Do you want it cleaned out or not?"

Then: "Kick at me like that a second time, and I'll leave you to go lame. You'll be lucky if you're good enough for stew. I've my misgivings that this head of yours will be worth anything—what is between these ears? Fluff?"

Meesahrah sighs and I hear her hooves stomping the dirt as she dances a little before everything settles, and a soft scraping noise starts.

"Can I chatter to you while you work?" I ask him.

"Chatter?"

"Talk."

"Certainly. With the way her ears are twitching, it seems Meesahrah here likes your voice. Shame it'll strain my beast's cognitive abilities to keep up. Be sure to use large words."

I grin in Meesahrah's direction. "How long have you had her?"

"Three long, *long,* trying, difficult, stubborn, challenging laps around the sun."

I'm silently laughing at the *way* he's saying the words. "What makes up a lap?"

"Six seasons turn over a lap here. How many seasons make up your world's span of time?"

"Wow, six, huh? We have four in a year."

He grunts. "Interesting. Do the seasons make for good planting and harvesting?"

"Two of them do in the part of the world I'm from. So what do you do here? As a job, I mean." I smile brightly. "Basically, pretend I'm an alien from another planet who has no concept of your planet's culture."

He chuckles. "I'll do my best to imagine such an unlikely scenario." The scraping stops and there's a shuffling sound, followed by a thump like something kicks out, and Breslin hisses, "I will *boil* that fluff!" before everything calms and the scraping takes up again. Easily, like his temper hasn't so much as twitched despite Meesahrah's testing it, he answers me. "I'm the Garthmaw. The breaker."

But *trainer* is the word my translator supplies for *Garthmaw.* "Like breaking... animals?"

His voice is unhurried and pleasantly relaxing as he takes the time to explain. "I break beasts. And don't judge my talents by Meesahrah, she's a special exception. An especially taxing, *special* exception. Get your teeth out of my face," he adds in the same tone, and I laugh because he delivers it so fluidly.

His voice holds laughter too when he continues. "In this culture, on this planet—let's say if you were an alien who was entirely unfamiliar with it," he teases, "we're largely settlements of farms and hunting plots.

To traverse this planet and to haul supplies on this planet—same as many other planets—we use docile, gentle, obedient, mostly intelligent individuals—"

There's another thumping sound and lots of shuffling, and I have to cover my mouth to stifle my laughter now.

Breslin's words come out evenly—perhaps a touch playfully—as everything settles down and he sets to scraping again, "As I was saying. We round up beasts to perform the incredibly important job of conveying goods and persons across vast distances."

"And it's your job to train these beasts."

He snorts. "Doesn't seem like I do well at it, does it?" There's a clap of rough hand on fleshy hind. "Even this thickskull can do a day's worth of work well. Don't let her fool you."

The smell has been intensifying the more he scrapes. It's probably much like a horse I suppose: all the dirt and grass and waste that collects inside a scoop-shaped hoof sort of ferments as it sits there and it has a particularly distinct, strong odor—not bad, just different. "She seemed to get us here just fine."

Again I hear the contact of his massive hand clapping in praise against Meesahrah's skin. "Credit where credit is due: Meesahrah here handled herself well in the storm, as always."

The last hoof is set on the floor and the little cracks and pops I hear remind me of the sounds my body makes after I've been sitting hunched over something. *"Done!"* Breslin declares, his voice an unintentional boom that has Kota startling a little right along with me.

"Feeling adventuresome?" he calls out, putting away his hoof-cleaning instruments from the sound of it.

"That depends. I'm currently on an unplanned space mission where I'm acting as a freelance ambassador—what else can we tackle in a day?"

He chuckles. "Ready to enter an alien's home?"

CHAPTER 10

BRESLIN

It doesn't take long for her to pace out my dwelling with me. My heart sinks as I realize that for as much as I take pride in my family home, I'd be clawing my way through the walls if I had to stay in this box all day. And that's what it has to seem like to her: four small walls with nothing more than a bed, a stove, a sink, a cupboard, and a relieving station in the corner.

Much to my discomfort, there's no door to the relieving station, just a flimsy curtain. That's all I've ever needed. I grew up using the outhouse, which still stands out back. But I don't want Sanna to have to attempt to navigate the overgrown path to the old insect-infested outhouse. And although she won't be able to see *me* in here, if she fails to seal the curtain around herself perfectly, I'll be able to see *her* and it's plain this fact makes her uncomfortable.

I rub the back of my neck, and wonder if I have the materials here to build a lightweight door. If I can build it on a sliding track we won't have to worry about the distance it will swing open—and that is a problem in a room of this size, which is why all I've ever fussed with is a curtain.

"It's a head game," she explains. "It shouldn't be any different to pull the curtain shut than it is to swing a door shut, but I can't *see* to be sure there isn't a gap in the curtain. I'll be fine, but I'm not going to lie: I'll be holding it in until you leave every day." She smiles up at me.

I tip my chin as something occurs to me. "From time to time, for various reasons, I'll see discomfort in my hooved companions, and it disturbs me if I can't determine why they feel it. With you, you can actually *tell* me. It's quite novel."

"I bet," she laughs softly.

Straightening, I drag my hand over my neck. "I'm sorry about this elimination situation. Do you need to relieve yourself right now?" I assume she must. I certainly do, but I believe I'll visit the outhouse and find out for myself what sort of shape it's in and what repairs it needs just in case Sanna uses it during her stay here.

She grimaces. "If you wouldn't mind..."

I pat her shoulder. "I'll be outside. I have a couple of animals to bed down for the evening and a few things I need to check on, so you'll have plenty of privacy." I move to leave, but seeing the puddle of water that's accumulated at my feet reminds me. "Before I forget, Ekan provided me a few sets of clothing he thought might fit you." I'd set the wax-paper wrapped bundle on my bed without a thought earlier, and now I cross to it and hand it to Sanna. "You'll have time to change into something dry while I'm gone too."

Her fingers touch my wrist cuff and skim my arm just above it. "Thank you, Breslin."

"You're welcome," I manage before I pull away from her warmth and drive myself out into the rain.

CHAPTER 11

SANNA

Breslin's muffled voice is cautious as he calls through the door, "Are you decent?"

Kota growls to warn me someone is talking to us through the door, as if I didn't know—but I have to admire her restraint. Normally she goes berserk and barks like someone is trying to use a battering ram instead of knocking. It'd be a little bit overkill for her to go nuts here when this isn't our house and the owner is in fact being nothing but extra polite. "You can come in!"

The door no more than shuts behind him when Breslin starts cursing. I catch a hissed, *"Ekan, you waste-stirring meddler!"*

"What?" My hand fumbles Kota's harness handle. "What's the matter?"

Instead of answering, Breslin mutters, "Let me change out of these wets and I'll fetch you a shirt of mine."

I look down at myself as if I can see what's wrong. "What am I wearing?" The outfit I'd picked out had fabric that felt like it would be comfortable enough to sleep in. The blousey top has a band that fits tighter around my chest so that it feels like a relaxed bra. Dread fills my stomach. I hate feeling stupid, or helpless, and I feel both of those things now as I wonder what I'm dressed in. I went to public school where kids with sight had no compunction about teasing the blind girl for the ugly style or color of her clothes. Some baggage never quite unpacks does it? The backs of my eyes start stinging.

"It's very pretty."

I blink my eyes until the stinging stops. "Then why...?"

I hear the wet plop of soaked clothes hitting the floor and I half turn out of courtesy even though I know he knows I can't see him.

"Let's just say what he gave you is... alluring."

I chew on the inside of my cheek and offer, "Let me look for something else."

"Don't bother," Breslin says. "I don't trust that Ekan provided you with anything that wasn't designed to make a man lose his mind."

Now I'm blinking for a whole different reason.

Breslin digs around in a drawer before he presses a soft shirt into my hands. I wonder if I should turn, or sit on the toilet and pull the curtain for privacy, but in the end decide to put his shirt on right here, right over my alluring, pretty clothes.

I'm in the middle of berating myself for being oddly relieved that Breslin doesn't see me as sexless, so it takes him two tries to get my attention. "Sorry," I say. "Try again."

"What does Kota need?"

I like that he cares enough to ask. "She eats meat and drinks water. And do you have something soft she can sleep on? Although she gets hot so she might choose the floor anyway..." I trail off as I consider again where *I'm* expected to sleep.

I've felt my way around the cabin twice. I'm very, very familiar with it: it's not very big. I know for a fact that there's only one bed.

Breslin moves around me, and I hear something with soft mass hit the floor with a hefty puff. "Bed," he says to himself more than us, "and I can put water in this," I hear the squeak of old hinges and the scrape of a dish being dragged out of the cupboard before the sound of running water reaches my ears. "Just need meat," he muses. "Will she eat stew?"

I worry my lip. "Let's try that, thank you."

I don't say anything more, and when he doesn't either, I wonder what he's waiting for.

Heat nears my skin and holds there a second, signalling his intention before his hand cups my elbow. "Sanna, I'm used to animals. Something seems to be nipping at you but I can't even begin to guess what *you* need. I like that you can talk to me, remember? So *tell* me: what's wrong?"

Something inside me loosens slightly. "You're absolutely right—and same for you. You'll have to be clear with what you... expect," I rush on, "but I was just thinking that no matter what we try to feed Kota, if it's too different from what she's used to, it could make her sick. I wasn't going to say that though since we unfortunately have no choice."

He gives my elbow a squeeze and it's ridiculously reassuring. "One step at a time. We'll see how she does on a small portion and hopefully she'll adjust just fine."

Another bowl is pulled out of the cupboard and I feel a rush of cool air before he says, "Ice box. There's always leftover food in here if you need it, although everything is bound to be quite a surprise for your system. We'll have to go easy with you too."

I hear a small *hissp* and I recognize the scent of flame. "Stove's heating our food...you drink water and eat stew too, yes?"

I grin. "Yes."

He exhales pure relief. "Good. Let me know what you think of the taste."

"Just as long as it's not Meesahrah," I tease.

He makes a dismissive noise but it's weighted with amusement. "No, no, for tonight I've decided she's all wrong for stew."

"Benevolent of you."

There's nowhere to sit. This is going to be tricky because I rarely stand while eating. It's too easy for me to tilt or drop my bowl or my cup. I suppose I could eat on the bed but I hate to drop crumbs or potentially spill things in places I'm intending to sleep so I stand at the stove with Breslin, listening to him stir.

I'm pleasantly surprised to reach out and find the counter is taller than the ones at home—it stands at nearly my elbow-height. This is good: I can work with this.

Breslin's quiet in a relaxed way that makes me think he's used to being alone. Instead of filling the time with nervous chatter, I focus on absorbing the sounds and smell and feel of things around me.

Something scrapes and from the motion of the sound I know Breslin is transferring our food to bowls. He warns, "This will be hot." Metallic clinks give me the impression he just plunked down spoons or the space-equivalent.

He asks, "Do you have a custom before we begin? Words of grace to your Creator?"

I'm surprised he thought to ask. "I do, actually, but I take care of my thanks inside my head. Do you have words you want to say out loud?"

"I give my words of appreciation inside my mind also, then I eat."

"Don't wait on me to start. It's going to take me a second to get oriented." I place my hands on the lip of the counter, my fingers almost relax-curled so that I can sense my space around me without accidentally knocking anything over. I begin exploring, slowly pushing my hands forward, careful to keep my palms resting on the counter surface, and when the fingers of my right hand bump into a utensil, I find and identify my spoon. My big, *big* spoon. I feel like a Goldilocks that settled in at the first cabin she came to. It's a silly thought that makes me smile, and I'm not worried: I can make do with big cutlery.

The glazed, round edge I encounter with the thumb of my left hand is the rim of my bowl—warm with the stew it contains—and when I go seeking a little further, the bottom edge of my cup nudges my right pinkie.

Unless cups are more animated here than they are at home, it had help. My lips curve up. "Thank you," I say to my silent observer.

"You're welcome," Breslin says quietly. *Easily.* He doesn't sound uncomfortable in a way that watching a blind person can cause some sighted people to grow apprehensive. Instead, in two words he manages to convey a tranquil sort of I'm-in-no-rush-observing-your-process as I learn my surroundings.

I trace my fingers up the cup's side to find it's more of a mug, which is even better. "Have you interacted with anyone like me before?" He's very easy to be around; his presence so laid back I don't feel self-conscious or on edge. I slip my hands through the very large handle, and bring it up to get a drink. When was the last time I had water? I don't know, but *I am thirsty.* So thirsty that despite noticing the giant's handle, I don't give the size of the mug a thought—and I should have. It's huge compared to what I'm used to, and the thicker edge clinks against my teeth.

"With the exception of the occasional Gryfala—how they manage to pick out the lookest Narwari yet *over*look their shockingly bad attitudes I'll never question, because it keeps me flush in jobs but *krit*—you're the first real alien I've entertained here. Unless Na'riths count, but I've known Ekan for an age and more moons than we have in our solar system."

I'm waiting for the word 'blind' to come up but... it doesn't.

Breslin took my question at face value: he sees me as an alien.

Not a *blind* alien.

Just... an alien.

Feeling refreshed to a degree that's surprising considering everything exhausting that's happened today—I dip my spoon into my soup, and take a taste. My tongue basically slathers around my bite and my stomach jumps in anticipation of my meal making it down. "This is *great.*"

"Good. I'm relieved you enjoy it." Breslin sounds pensive. "I was wondering what else would be to your liking. I'm afraid I have no reference; we'll have to do a bit of testing."

I'm three bites in before I can force myself to slow down enough to answer. "If it tastes like this, count me in for testing anything."

Breslin chuckles. "Excellent attitude."

More like excellent food. And a really, really nice host.

When we're done eating, Breslin asks if we want to brave the rain one last time to give Kota a chance to do her business.

He dons a slicker and gallantly helps me into mine, we squelch back into soggy footwear sans socks and the entire time I pace with Kota, I'm freezing up a little. Not from the temperature outside, but my nerves.

When we step back inside, Kota shakes herself off before Breslin can bring me a towel, but thankfully he's only stunned—not bothered. He's never cared for a furry being before, he tells me as he mops up the frigid spray of water. I apologize profusely, he brushes my apologies away, I unharness Kota and she lays down on the bed Breslin provided her.

I hang up my slicker, and try to fortify myself to approach the bed Breslin and I are going to share. I'm telling myself I have nothing to worry about, and I remind myself of some facts. Like, for example, how I wasn't aware of my outfit, but Breslin was—and with no prompting from me he chose to cover me in his shirt. It doesn't *seem* like the action of an alien who expects me to have sex with him. But sleeping in the same bed with a stranger—an *alien* stranger—it's an entirely different thing. At least, it could be. With Breslin... I might be way off, but I don't think he'd force me. I haven't gotten a danger vibe from him at all, and not a pushy one either. Does he have expectations he just hasn't voiced? Am I strong enough to stop him if he tries to force me?

Definitely not. But he hasn't once given me the impression that he'd do that. It's difficult to explain how, *why* I feel safe with an alien stranger but I trust Breslin not to do anything that could hurt me. I feel marginally sure that nothing is going to happen tonight other than sleeping.

Breslin speaks up from the other side of the room, his tone patient and I imagine he's been watching me think things through. "Ignore what you heard about being a bride. I didn't bring you home to breed on you."

A blush hits me at him using the word 'breed.' It helps to roll my eyes; my ridiculous blush fades and I manage to make it all the way to the bed, where I pull back the covers and climb in.

I listen to the thud of boots, the rustling of fabric, the sound his clothes make as they hit the floor. I wait for the drawer of dry clothes to open again, but it doesn't.

When the covers lift and weight dips the mattress, I feel like I'm strung tighter than a recurve bow.

I blurt, "I don't want to make this weird, but I didn't hear you..." My face is flaming.

"Didn't hear me what?"

"You're not wearing a shirt, are you?"

He snorts. "I'm not wearing a stitch."

I sit up. "You're *naked?*" I squeak.

The mischief content in his words is 100-proof. "Woman, it's not as if you can see anything."

I gasp and a quake of laughter attacks me. "You did *not* just say *that!*"

The bed creaks under his bulk as he makes himself comfortable and it shudders when he falls back. "If you can hear that I didn't dress for bed, you heard me tease you perfectly." He pats the round of my blanket-covered hip. "Sleep, salk. The days here start early."

I thought I'd be wide awake, tense and waiting to be pounced on no matter what the alien who I was gifted to says, but I'm smiling as my head hits the soft pillow. The last thing I remember thinking is that my pillow smells nice. *Piña colada and a fresh basket of chips at my favorite Mexican restaurant.*

It smells just like Breslin.

CHAPTER 12

BRESLIN

"Crite, are you dead?" I pick up one of her hands and drop it, watching it flop bonelessly to the bed.

I grab her smooth shoulder and shake her.

Kota shoves against my leg, fur bristling. Her lips peel back to reveal an upper and lower set of sparkling, sharp teeth. Her eyes are a darker shade than her owner's—which seems fitting because unlike Sanna's sweet gaze, Kota's focused glare promises me all sorts of pain if I dare to handle her mistress in such a way again.

I give her a patient look. "I'm not hurting her."

Kota is unconvinced.

I wiggle Sanna's limp hand. "Is she always like this? What if you have an emergency? What happens when you need to go outside?" Not taking my eyes off of the animal staring me down, I call, *"Sanna."*

No response from the human. *Has she fallen into some kind of coma?* I shout, "SANNA."

Kota strongly disapproves of me shouting at her human. She demonstrates this fact by lunging at me with a roar.

The sound of her pet is what sparks Sanna to regain consciousness. "K-kota?" Disoriented, still half asleep, her elbow buckles and she plants face-first into the bed on her first attempt to rise.

Kota wheels her attention to her person, bumping her oddly-textured nose into the underside of Sanna's hand.

"Hey, Kota," Sanna mumbles.

"Good rising to you, Sanna."

Instantly, she stiffens. Heartbreaking dismay crosses her face a moment before she attempts a smile. She murmurs a hoarse, "Not just a dream, huh?"

Tentatively, I stroke the back of her hand. "I didn't mean to give you a rough waking, but I'll be out to do chores and I could be gone for sticks if I have to go to the far pasture. I didn't want you to wake and not be able to find me."

"Sorry you had to wait on me—I can't believe I slept so hard. Thank you..." She slaps the side of her face three times, making me jolt.

It must assist humans' mandible function in the morning because her lips work better at making her words clear when she asks, "Can we go with you?"

I've already drawn on my boots and am tugging my coat off its hook, well able to hear the Narwari impatiently hollering for me to bring them their breakfast. "I'm afraid we have to hurry, but I'd be glad to have your company," I tell her.

Sanna pushes up from the bed and feels her way to the relieving station. I step outside to wait, and at her call of, "Done!" I reenter, and dig about for daywear clothes and a coat for her while she washes her hands. Then I find us something to take the edge off early hunger on our way to the barn.

The set of Sanna's brows and the purse of her lips as she dries off her hands gives me pause. "What does this human expression mean?" I ask, and take her fingers.

Soap is harsh here. It's got enough grit in it to scrub the belly off a gremhoc—or a Garthmaw's hands clean. Farm life has a way of making soap with this potency frequently necessary. But it's scoured Sanna's skin raw, and at most she's used it twice. "That won't do," I murmur, and keep hold of her hand as I step backwards and pull moisturizing salve off the one shelf I have in this place. "This will be good for your skin. We'll need to make you more suitable soap."

"*Thank* you," she says, coating her hands before she slips into her shoes, and fits Kota with her harness.

I wonder if skin like hers will need frequent applications of salve all over. It's so soft; it must take a great deal to keep it hydrated. Sanna might enjoy helping me make more. After chores will be the time to bathe, and after that perhaps we can spend time at the stove. Might as well make our meal at that time too.

I find I'm looking forward to spending time with her.

I press the fruit I've been holding for Sanna into her hand with a grunted, "Food," and help her into her coat.

With that, we set off for the barn. I gaze around at the gently rolling hills that surround us and at the peaceful scene that a pack of Narwari work so hard to project. I don't know what Sanna's land is like, but I've no doubt she's as rooted to hers as I am to mine and it would be difficult to be ripped away from it all.

I can't reverse her capture, but I can do my best to be a good host and make her stay pleasant. I want Sanna to be happy while she's here. "Chatter to me," I tell her.

"What?" Sanna asks before a laugh bells from her, causing Kota to look up at her sharply. "Yeah, I can do that."

"It's good to see you smiling," I tell her. "I thought I all but had a corpse in my bed. I was rearranging my day, thinking as soon as you stopped breathing, I was going to have to drop everything and bury you."

She laughs again. "I said I was sorry! I don't normally sleep that hard, I swear!"

"So you say, so you say; eat your fruit." I hide my grin as I bite into mine.

"I'm not awake enough to deal with you," she vows as she sniffs her food. "Smells good. What is this?"

"It grows from the trees here. It has sweet flesh and it's filling. You just crunch through the skin. Yes, like that," I coach.

"Do I eat the skin too?" she asks, her cheek puffing out with her mouthful.

"You do, and when you find the part that feels a bit like a jelly?"

"Scared here, but listening. What do I do with it?"

"Eat that. It's good for you."

"Yes, boss," she answers dutifully. "Is there a way I can help you with chores?"

Boss? My translator supplies *foreman,* which is confusing as I have no authority over a worksite. "I've been wondering the same," I tell her. "Each Narwari gets a measure of extruded pellet. You can measure out the scoops and fill their buckets for me."

"I can do that," she confirms, and the relief smoothing across her features tells me this is important to her. Either she desires to earn her keep or desires to keep herself far from boredom, I'm not sure, but I can imagine I'd feel much the same if I were in her place. I turn over various chore possibilities in my mind as we make our way to the barn.

Meesahrah is the first of the Narwari to greet Sanna—she greets Kota too, though Kota looks wary despite Meesahrah's welcoming warble-calls.

The rest of the pack appears startled at the newcomers, but that doesn't stop the lot of them from assembling themselves in a stalking formation. A sharp hiss from me breaks them up.

It also spooks Sanna and Kota, both of whom jump.

"My apologies," I say quickly. "They were starting to get a little brazen and I didn't want them to hurt you."

"Ah," Sanna says, and raises her bucket. "Just tell me where to stand with this then and I'll—"

The pack zeroes in on the fact that their would-be prey is actually a meatgrain-giver, and their behavior melts to that of orphans, all beginning to bawl at her like she's their long lost mother.

"Beggars," I mutter and shoo them back. "Where's your manners? Line up."

Begrudgingly, they all do, and Sanna holds up the first bucket.

I tell her, "Cohrah is approaching you, she's the salk leader of this pack—"

Meesahrah shoves her way up from the end of the line. In three laps of the sun, she's never shown a flicker of interest in interacting with the pack, but now she is bolder than even the leader salk. She knows who Sanna and Kota are, but even so—it's unusual. "I retract that. Meesahrah is claiming the right to feast first."

"Good morning, Meesahrah," Sanna coos, and Kota tilts her head first one way, then the other, before she emits a sharp sound of protest.

The Narwari scatter—except for Meesahrah, who buries her snout in the bucket.

"You're still my best girl, Kota," Sanna says. "Don't scare them away from their food."

Kota sits and I could be imagining it but her eyes seem to narrow thoughtfully as she watches the pack reassemble themselves behind Meesahrah.

Sanna sends an apologetic smile in my direction, only a little off center of me as she explains, "Kota isn't a classically trained guide dog. Certified schools produce excellent animals but my family raises this breed," she nods down to the animal with its unique pattern and angular features, "And I was there when Kota's litter was born. Kota was the pup I wanted so we trained her ourselves. We did all the research and worked through years of training together but... she's very much got her own mind."

My brow flattens as I look at the animal of mine that's leaning hard against the fence, mannerlessly shoving her muzzle into the bucket Sanna's clutching. "I can assure you I sympathize," and I say this in such a forbearing, flat tone that Sanna snickers.

"If you reach out," I tell Sanna, "and feel along Meesahrah's neck—"

Sanna adjusts the bucket so she can hold it in one hand, and places her other on Meesahrah's neck crest. "Okay..."

"Feel the tassels?"

Sanna takes hold of the strings of tassels. "Yes."

"All the trained Narwari wear them. You can catch any of the trained ones and ride them if you have to."

Sanna drops her hand back to the bucket, gripping it. "Ride them? I don't know how to ride!"

"I think you might learn," I muse.

"I think you might be crazy," she informs me. "They seem kind of tall."

"What's your point?"

"I'm kind of not good with heights!" Sanna half-wails, and Kota sends me a scathing look and her fur puffs out just as it did when she thought I was harming her mistress. I reach down to offer her a reassuring pat, but she bares her teeth at me.

I raise my eyes skyward. *Save me from temperamental females.*

Meesahrah finishes her bucket and promptly reaches down to Sanna's feet to nip out of the next one.

"Enough for you before you catch gut bloat," I warn, and motion for Cohrah to step forward.

Eyes slitted at Meesahrah, Cohrah makes her way for her bucket as Sanna raises it and waits. When Cohrah's nose dives into the food, Sanna reaches out and brushes her hand along Cohrah's tassels.

"These feel pretty," she remarks.

"Just imagine how they'll feel under your hands as you ride."

"It's the falling part I don't think I'll like," she complains.

"Bah. That's what everybody says."

Sanna gapes at me. "Maybe that should tell you something!"

I laugh. "That's what everybody says *at first.*"

"And then what? After you fall you suddenly change your mind?" she asks in disbelief.

She goes still as I lean in, cheek brushing hers. "Sometimes," I whisper, "the ride is worth the fall."

CHAPTER 13

SANNA

"What's next?" I ask Breslin as we stack the empty, rinsed buckets back in the barn.

"Hold still," he murmurs, and I do when I feel his fingers touch my hair, and something long and thin slides slowly along my scalp before he pulls it free.

"What is it?" I ask, ducking.

"Bit of hay. No need to cower."

I straighten immediately and pretend to scowl. "Me? Cowering? Never."

"Hmm," he says. "The storm knocked trees down. I need to ride the fenceline and repair any damage before we have a case of wandering Narwari, and the neighbor's grazing thieves start disappearing."

I rub Kota's ear. "What does the end part of that statement mean?"

Another bucket clacks on the pile as Breslin takes the last one from my other hand. "Closest neighbor is three sticks away."

"Okay. Let's pretend I understand that." Then I shake my head. "Actually, no. I need help. 'Three sticks away' sounds like distance, but you use 'stick' like it's... like it's a way to tell actual time, like a few minutes or something. What IS a stick?"

He sounds like he's smiling. "A stick."

"That's great. *Thanks.*"

His answer is a rumbling chuckle. It's nice. "You haven't known all this time?"

Kota brushes against me as she adjusts her stance. A guide dog learns to be patient but alert during people-conversation, and she's settling in. "I was too entertained by your alien ways to actually find out."

"That's it. Now you have to try a stick for sure."

"*Try* a stick...?" I'm so confused.

Breslin's finger and thumb tap my mouth. "Open." He waits until I stop pulling back from the surprise of it—and he presses something that feels like a thin chopstick between my teeth. It tastes a little like licorice.

"This," he guides my chin down a little at the same time he tugs my jaw so that I'm craning my neck up for him, "Is a timestick." His breath fans across my face as he gets closer. "And it looks like your teeth are much like mine, with flat molars."

Did he just check *my* teeth? "Yethsss..." I manage to say around the stick.

"Very good—now bite down. On a being of my size, the length from our back molar to our lips is a *nick of a stick,* or *stick* for short."

"O-okay..."

"As time passes, you come to half a stick, then to three quarters of a stick, and finally, you gnaw away until you reach an end of a stick." His hand closes around my arm and he brushes his thumb over my skin reassuringly, like *See?*

I'm not quite sure I do. "How long does it take until you're through with a stick?"

"A length of a stick."

"But... how long is that?"

He slides another chopstick along my hand. "That long."

Consternation fills me.

I grasp the chopstick in my palm so we're both holding it. "Where does the stick *go?* Are you *ingesting* it? A stick?"

"Your kind don't gnaw on anything?"

"Well, only, like gum or something. Not sticks—"

Toothpicks.

"Okay," I correct, "I've heard some people chew on something like this but where I'm from, products made from wood aren't edible."

"Not all of our trees are. This variety is."

This variety is also tasty and it goes a long way towards explaining why this has remained a method of telling time. I'd eat candy to measure time too. Is gnawing on a stick bad for teeth here? Surely not.

"What if someone chews fast?"

"You can't chew fast. It's a stick."

"It seems imprecise..." I shrug.

"What method do your people use for measuring time?"

"Hours. Those are made up of sixty minutes. Minutes are made up of sixty seconds."

He seems thoughtful. "And they're uniform then?"

"Like clockwork... ha—Earthens would get that pun. It's precise and we keep time on clocks. But if we don't have our phones or watches we can count *one Mississippi, two Mississippi,* and so on, and each time you finish saying *Mississippi,* a second has passed."

"Does every Earthen speak at the same speed?"

I grin. "I get where you're going with this question. I mean, ours isn't the *same,* but I get it: everyone's got their ways." I motion towards him with my hand. "I interrupted. You were saying you needed to check fences before your grazing thieves disappear?"

He makes a humor-filled noise of assent even as he says, "Not mine. The neighbor's herd of llarrolla roam far and wide and lean right up against my fences to eat up everything green they can reach. A good fence keeps us good neighbors, but if it's down and his llarolla wander over... you can see where that would cause bad blood."

"They'd eat your Narwari's grass, and your Narwari would have no food."

The bucket clacking stops. "Halt there: you are far off the path," Breslin says, and my concentration shifts to my feet thinking he means that I'm literally off of a path in the barn until he explains, "The Narwari don't eat grass. They *pretend* to eat grass. Unsuspecting herd animals are drawn to peaceful-looking Narwari packs, and my Narwari do as they do in the wild and lure prey in and decimate them. The neighbor won't fault me if the Narwari manage to coax a llarolla or two to their death if his animals are sneaking under my fence—I've done all I can by penning my pack in. But if my fence is down then my pack has an unfair advantage against their prey."

"That is so disturbing."

"The neighbor would agree with you. Thus, I best get out and check that fence."

"Can I go with you?"

When Breslin's quiet, I'm afraid he's trying to think of a polite way to tell me I'm a hindrance. "Breslin," I reach out and find his arm, my fingers bumping over his metal wrist bracer before smoothing over his rough skin. "Back home, I've worked so hard for independence. I've had to prove to everyone I can do things—I can do almost anything if people give me a chance. You told me to tell you what I need. Well? I can't sit still. It'll legit drive me crazy. I'll drive *Kota* crazy. I can walk around here if you'd rather me do that, but if there's a way to stay busy, please tell me how."

His voice holds approval when he says, "Industrious to the core. If your people are all like you, they'd get along very well with Iechydmaw."

His people. If his people are all like him, then humans would get along really well with the Iechydmaw too.

Women for sure. There's just something about Breslin that makes me want to be near him.

He brings his hand over his arm, trapping my hand over his skin. "I wasn't going to tell you no. I was turning over whether you should work on driving or riding today."

I really, really don't want to climb up on a very tall carnivorous alien lifeform but this is my chance to show Breslin that I can be more than mobile decoration. I don't flinch. "And what did you decide?"

"Brave salk," he murmurs.

My translator says, *Brave girl.*

I adopt my most innocent face, the 'aw, shucks,' earnestly helpful one. "I could be wrong, but since I've already been started on wagon basics, it might be quicker for you to get me rolling with that so you'll have enough time to check out your fenceline."

He clucks his tongue. "That's a fair thought, and rather works in favor of someone who's too nervous to ride."

I bite my bottom lip and borrow his noncommittal, *"Hmm."*

He chuckles as he strolls out of the barn to fetch me a Narwari.

CHAPTER 14

SANNA

Kota and I are pacing the pasture connected to the barn where Breslin's untacking Cohrah after my 'driving lesson.'

We're surrounded by Narwari. I've been in horse pastures before where the sounds of languid, quiet grazing add a peaceful hum to the air.

There's no quiet munching here. No harmless grinding of greens over flat teeth.

When my hand had been inside of Meesahrah's mouth, I'd felt the sharpness of her teeth, but I hadn't imagined that she was less a horse and more a crocodile that only *pretends* at being a horse long enough to catch a zebra.

Shivvver.

They seem nice enough animals though. The driving lesson was actually really fun. And though there were plenty of downed trees we had to navigate the cart around, the fence line was thankfully undamaged which makes Breslin's life easier. His time is best spent on training instead of repairs.

Whenever I reach out to touch a Narwari, I find their heads lowered as they deceitfully meander with their noses to the ground. As long as I don't think about why they're doing it, it's just as relaxing as strolling through a herd of equine or something equally as placid. The worst that's happened to me with these guys was me getting too close to a set of hindquarters, and I got whipped by a surprisingly strong, thin tail.

Behind me, a steady tread of hoof on soft ground follows me, and I smile, having an idea of who is keeping pace.

When a long jaw drops over my shoulder, Kota stops walking. So do I.

I reach out and catch the tasselled collar, feeling along their number and finding their pattern (four strung in a row, a gap, and four more) to be Meesahrah's, just like I'd thought. Releasing Kota's harness handle, I stroke the Narwari's neck, enjoying the way she heaves a sigh and leans into my touch. Since she seems willing, I give in to my curiosity, bringing my hands over her, learning her slowly. Then I move to stand further along her side, reach up on my tip toes and stretch to pet along her spine. "That alien is bonkers if he thinks I'm going to climb up here," I tell her.

"I didn't mean *that* one," Breslin says from beside me.

I choke and Kota whines and in my moment of distraction, Meesahrah reaches around and snatches my forearm.

Breslin roughly claps his hands together, startling us both—not to mention Kota, who wuffs at him. It's less than a bark and more of a disapproving woof.

Meesahrah drops my arm reluctantly and I breathe a sigh of relief that, once again, she didn't actually use any of those sharp teeth on me.

"This one is a challenge even for me," Breslin explains. "We'll start you on a nice one."

Meesahrah honks and he replies with a pointed, "You know it's true."

I snicker at them.

"Don't think I haven't seen that dog of yours leading you around," Breslin says to me.

"You know she has to!" I protest, finding it difficult to speak because my diaphragm is spasming with a chuckle. "It's her *job.*"

Breslin growls—that popping growl-sound again, but it's a relaxed, more faux-contemplative noise that makes my skin tighten in an unexpected way. "Mmhmm, I'd wager Meesahrah would say leading me around is her job too. Just ask her. I'll wait."

I snicker harder.

"You want to claim to me that yours doesn't do the running roughshod over you sort of leading? None of that dutifully-doing-her-job partnered to you, leading."

"Never," I lie.

"Don't rouse me to call you the names I keep stored up for Meesahrah."

Keeping one hand wrapped over Kota's harness I clap the other against my leg. "Oooh, tell me: what's the next insult you had in mind for her?"

"I thought I might go with double-tongued, hook-beaked moldwarp," he says thoughtfully. Over my laughter, he changes the subject, but he sounds like he's smiling. "When you're ready, your first ride can be on Cohrah. For now, let's head back so we can wash up and eat. Tomorrow after chores I need to take a trip to the neighbor to the east. The round of training and hoof trims must go on, though I don't believe I'll take on new clients this season. Would you like to come along?"

"I would."

"Then tomorrow after we finish chores, we'll eat, have baths, and we'll leave right after."

"Wait, baths? I'm scared to hope but like we get the full splish-splash *bath*-baths?" I clutch onto Kota's harness handle to stop myself from jumping up and down.

Breslin makes a puff-snort—it's not as harsh as a real snort, and it's infused with a heaping measure of humor. "I don't know how they do it where you're from, but here, a bath means we heat water, fill the tub, and we scrub up." He moves past me, but the sound of his voice stays pointed in my direction, making me think he's throwing the offer over his shoulder, "You can even bathe first. Would you approve?"

"I would *very* much approve, why thank you. Forward, Kota." We start to follow him out of the paddock when something catches me from behind.

Having a fair idea of who it is, I go still and slowly reach up to find Meesahrah's nose, and below that is the bunched nape of my coat clamped between her lips. My fingers trace past her fangs and follow the line of a mischievous *smile.*

"You're going to get in trouble," I warn her.

Her lips inch along my coat, sucking more of the fabric into her mouth before she gives it a playful yank, making me gasp as I fall back a step. Kota goes *wild.* Barking madly, she's not playing—she's worried.

Breslin bellows, "MEESAHRAH!"

His boots sound almost as heavy as a Narwari's steps as he barrels for us and Meesahrah wisely releases me a second before he reaches her.

CLONK!

It's hard to say, but I think these aliens just clashed heads.

"We *talked* about this," Breslin intones with great emphasis. "You're going to have to find someone in the pack to tease—not the guests, Meesahrah. *Never* the guests." He does a lot of growling, and only some of the words translate which means, I think, that he's mostly cussing her out.

At the end of what seems like a stern tongue lashing involving words harsher-sounding than mere hook-beaked moldwarps, Meesahrah moos—but even to my ears, it sounds less than genuine, and definitely not very trustworthy.

Kota must be of the same mind too because she mutters a low grumble, the dog version of *You better watch yourself.*

CHAPTER 15

SANNA

Frustration tries to ignite inside my muscles but I take a deep breathe, relax, and try to think. I was sure I set Kota's harness on the little cubby next to the bed. I feel around for it one more time before I kneel and start systematically sweeping the floor with my hands, making sure no area around me is missed—making sure that nothing *in* the area around me is missed.

Breslin calls, "Can I come in? Morning chores are done and I'm ready for a thaw-out. It's colder out here than Meesahrah's heart."

My concentration shatters because I can't help but laugh. "Yeah! Come in, I'm dressed. Thanks for asking."

"Of course—" Breslin starts, but his easy-going words die, all traces of humor chased off by concern. "What the krit happened that you're on the floor?"

"I'm not hurt or anything. I just can't find Kota's harness. I try to put everything in the same place to avoid losing stuff—"

"Sanna?"

"Yeah?" I scoot my hands further away from me, canvassing more area. "I'm sure it's right out of my reach but I can't—"

"Said true—it is just out of your reach: Kota has it."

"She... *what?*" I exclaim, shock bubbling up. "You are so busted! You got me good, you sneak!"

Kota's tail thumps guiltily. Dogs can have a guilty tailwag—this one sure does.

"I don't follow. What alien element am I missing in order to understand this conversation?" Breslin muses.

I crawl to Kota's bed. "This isn't the first time I've 'lost' Kota's harness here—last night when you went out to do the last check on the Narwari? I went to walk Kota but I couldn't find her harness. I thought maybe I'd knocked it off the cubby or something. Finally I asked Kota to help me, and she brought it to me. I spent forever telling her what a smart, beautiful girl she is. The smartest girl *ever*," I stress as Kota's tail beats out a faster (guiltier) rhythm.

"Oh I bet she liked that," Breslin offers.

"She did! And two treats out of the fridge—"

"Crite, she's good."

"Right? Then I played with her outside—"

"My dear salk, no; she played you—but go on."

My fingers catch on the harness Kota's clutching half-under her chest with the 'H' strap held in her grinning mouth. Yes, she's definitely grinning—her lips are pulled all the way back and up and her tail's still going.

"You said this started when?"

Kota stretches out her leg to help me fit her harness on, standing when I need to clip it around her chest. "Yesterday, why?"

"Well I'm no expert in Earthen lifeforms but she looked a bit left out when you were learning to drive. Perhaps there's no connection, but if there is, she may need reassurance."

I lean on her and tug her big ear over my mouth like a megaphone—but I whisper into it. "You're my best girl, Kota."

Her ear flicks my lips, proabably because me talking into it tickles the heck out of her. I dig my fingers into the fur of her shoulders and scratch.

This is where Kota would normally groan and beg for more but when the harness goes on, she's in work mode, and as far as she's concerned, we're on the clock now and it's time to be serious. "Toilet time?" I ask her.

But she knows. As soon as I'm up and my hand is on the harness she's ready to go. As we exit, pots clang. Breslin told me we'd be boiling water and it sounds like he's getting it ready.

To think he has to go to all that work every time he wants to really scrub himself.

When Kota and I get back, buckets clack, a kettle squeals sounding just like a teapot from home, and the room is so damp and warm I can feel steam gently mist my skin. Kota starts panting but she's as curious about this process as I am. Breslin sets me to the job of bucket-filling. He does the emptying, but I tell him when the bucket is full.

"Where are you putting this water?" I ask.

"Off to your left about perhaps six of your paces you'll find a metal tub."

"Where did the tub come from?" There's definitely been no bathtub in here.

"It hangs on the wall when it's empty and dried."

"Gotcha. This bucket's ready," I tell him, and Breslin brushes against me as he lifts the pail and empties it into one of the pots on the stove. When the other one starts squealing, he pours the boiling water into our bath. Our pails aren't that big, so when he offers, "You can start now; I'll get the wagon loaded while you do," I'm thinking *how much water am I washing up in, exactly?* "Then I'll scrub up, we clear out and we go. Follow me?"

"I follow you but... it doesn't sound like the tub's full yet."

"It isn't full—that would take half the morning if you want heated water, and it cools off mighty fast. We—"

"No, that's fine, I just had a different mental picture. I'm all for Pioneer bathing, alien-style."

Before he can leave the farmhouse, I ask, "What do I use to empty the tub? Is there like a hose attachment to drain it, or are we doing it by bucket? And where do we dump the water?"

"After you bathe, I'll bathe, and then we'll get to the part where we empty the water pail by pail."

I pause, my hand resting between Kota's velvety ears. "This is like old Earth isn't it? Where everyone in the house shares bathwater until it's mud?"

I hear him gathering things together as he gets closer to the door. "Surely you aren't that filthied." He sounds completely unworried. "And if you are, it still might be good enough to mop the floors with later."

"Right," I agree weakly.

Mopping floors. With dirty bathwater. *Welcome to alien farmlife.*

After I wash up and dress (as it turns out, Ekan did pack a few skirts and tops that I can wear in public) and call Breslin in, Kota and I take a short walk in the Narwari pen. I asked Breslin to call for us when he's done so that I can help empty the buckets—and to mop the floors with the water that we stewed ourselves in, mmm.

Breslin does exactly as he promised and bellows loud enough the Narwari mini-stampede around us and I could be way off, but I think Meesahrah purposely uses herself as a shield to block the other Narwari from bumping us until they calm down.

When Kota and I make it back to the house, Breslin's halfway done emptying water so I waste no time in grabbing a bucket and beginning the process of hauling it to the door. We form sort of an old-style fireman's line of two people, one to pull the water and one to dump it outside near the dormant garden.

Once finished, I find out there's just the one mop, which makes sense since Breslin lives alone, but he must whip that thing over the floors at ninety miles an hour because he calls, "Done!" before I can finish asking him if I can take over.

After the mop water is dumped in the garden, we stand in the farmhouse that smells surprisingly fresh (and a little like freshly wet dog and wet Narwari) and absorb our accomplishment.

"You look very fetching in that skirt," Breslin says.

"Thanks; I feel weird because I haven't shaved my legs in forever. At home, I'd just wear pants."

I find out it's possible to hear someone's—somealien's—shock. "You *shave* your *legs?*"

"If I'd known I was going to have to wear a skirt? Definitely."

Something brushes me; I have a second to register *this feels like his shoulder* before the big meaty thing moves into me and my hands land on his back because Breslin's taken up the hem of my skirt, bared my leg, and hooked my ankle over his knee for an examination of my limb.

I huff, "You're *such* a farrier."

Kota wuffs and her claws tap along the floor as she shuffles uncertainly.

Breslin sounds far off in thought as he examines the knobby part of my ankle bone. "Why do you say that?"

I twist a little to wave at myself. "Because you just grabbed my foot off the floor like it was a hoof!"

His shoulder shifts away briefly before settling back, almost like a human shrugs. "If you didn't like it you could have kicked at me."

"Oh please. Would that have even slowed you down?"

He snorts. "If I let a little kicking stop me I'd be out of job. Why must you shear your legfur? It's very fine," he remarks, stroking my leg like one might a strange but interesting animal.

I try to politely ignore the feelings of interest his innocent touch immediately stokes, and focus on his question. "It's not 'fur'—it's hair—and where I'm from it's considered... unsightly, I guess."

"Well, San San, you're here now, where no one will form a like or dislike of you based on the filaments that grow on your limbs."

San San? I melt even as I snicker. "My limbs? As if I have so many. It's just my legs."

"No..." Breslin says carefully. "There is hair growth along your arms too."

I full out laugh. "Yes but nobody cares about that. *Under* my arms though; that's a different story."

"*Whoa.*" He leans away a little and says the word in the way he uses it to halt his alienhorse. "You mean to tell this Garthmaw that you go to the trouble of shearing your leg hair, only to leave the hair intact on your arms—yet you worry about the fluff that stays hidden *under* your upper limbs which are covered *under* clothes?"

"It's not as ridiculous as you make it sound."

"I beg to differ," his voice is almost faint amid his confusion. "Who will even know it's there?"

"Well at home, other people would see."

"Why would they care?"

"I don't know."

"Who are these people? Who has the time to notice?"

"I guess it's noticeable? I get what you're saying, and it's not like I notice it on other women."

"Then if it doesn't bother you, why would you care if they care?"

"I don't... I know it sounds nuts." My fingertips catch on one of his cheek grooves. I've wondered about these things ever since he let me learn his face that first day. Maybe these grooves are common features on his people. Or he could be horribly, tragically disfigured—but all I feel is interesting texture. I haven't asked him because I don't care what he looks like. In all the ways that matter, Breslin is beautiful.

And evidently he doesn't have leg hair. Or if he does, he sure doesn't cut it.

His fingers close over mine, catching my hand over his face to capture my attention. "I know a little of shearing animals. How does a human shave?"

"I sit down so I don't kill myself and I take a razor and—carefully—run it over my hairy spots."

"If it would make you comfortable, I'll fetch you a razor."

Under his hand where he's keeping me pressed to his face, I manage to pat his cheek. "You're right; no one will care here. I'll be fine."

"I want you to be at ease. Let's take the hair off."

"Wait, 'lets?' Are we doing this together now?"

"You've piqued my curiosity. I confess I want to watch an alien shear her leg fur."

My leg is still propped over his knee, and he's sort of holding me as he admits this sudden desire. This is so strange.

But he's done so much for me. Until this, he hasn't gotten close to asking for anything and I find I want to give him something back—even if it is just letting him watch me shave. "Is the blade you're familiar with basically a long, sharp, sharp knife?"

"Of course."

"Like for man's face?"

He leans away from me but unconsciously tightens our hands to his jaw. "For a man's *face?!*"

I chortle at his reaction. "Where I'm from, men shave their faces."

"Your kind sound like they have an obsession with cutting what grows naturally. Next you'll tell me you cut your mane hair."

"Well..."

He drops my hand. "Crite, I knew it."

I scritch Kota behind the ears, feeling her raise her head higher when Breslin speaks then turning towards me when I talk. "Forget your horror at the oddness of human customs for just a moment, your alienfeelings aren't important right now—"

"You sass-mouthed mite."

He delivers this with no heat, and I'm grinning as I finish. "—I don't know how to safely use a straight razor. Do you think *you* can do it without cutting me? You'd only have to do it up to my knees."

He's aghast. "You trust me to shear you?"

"Okay, I wasn't going to say anything, but my people call it shaving."

"Oh. When we take off a fur blanket without its hide skin we call it shearing."

Now *I'm* aghast. "It's a fur BLANKET?!"

"Well," he stammers adorably, "Maybe more like small pelts—"

I wail.

Kota howls.

Breslin drops my foot, releasing me from my 'hoof'-check. "Enough, enough: cease squalling—I'm getting the blade. Seat yourself and stop that loathsome noise."

I snicker into Kota's neck and she pants happily.

LEGS SHAVED—NO NICKS, just one slightly stressed alien who for all his curiosity, could only bring the blade up to my mid-calf without balking (he said his nerves couldn't take de-pelting and he'd heard about laser technologies being tested in his capital, and maybe they'd like to de-hair an alien leg or two)—we're ready to roll out of the farm yard.

I'm full of curiosity during our first foray together to a training and hoof trimming appointment. It officially kicks off with Meesahrah jostling Cohrah out of the way for the privilege of pulling our wagon, and Breslin oversees more driving practice for me as he directs me to our destination.

I love driving. It's second only to walking Kota.

When we pull up at an area that changes from gravel crunching under our tires—ah, make that wagon wheels—to softer grass that lets the wheels sink a little, Breslin tells me to call a stop to Meesahrah.

I'm taking in the smells (more Narwari) and sounds (honking Narwari) when I hear Meesahrah start snapping her teeth.

Breslin quietly warns, "Don't you dare."

A new voice calls, "Ah, Meesahrah. Being pleasant as alway—krit, is that a *woman?*"

The wagon edges forward and the reins go taut in my hands and when Meesahrah's fangs scissor together again, Breslin brings his hand down heavily on the seat, making it vibrate under us as he growls, "Bite him and I will fashion your teeth into jewelry for Sanna to wear."

"Don't bring me into this. Hi," I wave to the stranger. Kota shifts beside my leg and I can tell she's waving her paw too.

"Well hello, beauty," he pauses in that way people do when they're regarding someone, "And beasts. Something the matter, Breslin?" he says by way of greeting.

Breslin doesn't say anything back.

The stranger doesn't seem to notice. His attention seems to be caught up in other things. "If I didn't know better, she almost looks like a Gryfala. I've heard a Garthmaw attracts rare treasures, but crite! What can you tell me about the lovelies you've brought?"

"Sanna?" Breslin says slowly. "This was Fellmoor."

...Was?

Breslin does not extend the greeting *Fellmoor, this is Sanna,* like I expect. Maybe his culture doesn't add this particular nicety.

Or maybe Breslin's beyond the ability to be polite. His words sound like they have fangs longer than Meesahrah's. "Sanna, hold my trimmers." Something heavy shudders as he drags it from where it rested near my feet before it's weight is laid across my lap. "I just sharpened the blades on these. We should all be careful. They'll cut clean through anything that dares to stick out." Another heavy item is dragged past my foot. "And here's the emasculator. Any salkell needing to be controlled around salks can be fixed right with these. Will they be needed this visit, Fellmoor?"

I set my hand on the bench between us, my little finger brushing Breslin's thigh. His voice sounds warning-tense, no teasing—he's not fondly annoyed like he was with Meesahrah. Not fond at all.

Two of Breslin's big fingers tap the back of my hand twice, and it's mostly reassuring. Nobody's died yet.

Fellmoor sounds like he shuffles back and his voice turns flat. "What the krit crawled in your boot? If anyone needs controlling it's not me. Crite! You've been in the business of intimidating poor beasts too long; next you'll pull out the hoofrasp and warn me that it works on stones."

There's a metallic snap. The emasculator?

Fellmoor sighs gustily. "Message received. You can quit swinging around your kritted tool."

Breslin relaxes, and despite the somewhat inauspicious start, Breslin's humor returns as he works on the first Narwari. Listening to him is a treat; he's got a *really* nice, smooth voice and eventually even though his words and commands are meant for an animal, I have to fan myself when he rumbles, "Don't panic love; I'm mounting up now. Goood, there's a good salk, *yes.*"

I shift on the seat and Kota who had been panting up at me goes abruptly silent, her breath-puffs no longer hitting my arm. I ghost my fingertips over her muzzle, and find she's biting her lip; that's what cut off her breathing. This is her quizzical look. It's like she's wondering what the heck is going on with me.

That makes two of us. This alienman is just trying to do his job and I have no business reacting to him, geez.

Without warning, the wagon rolls forward.

"MEESAHRAH, *STAY.*"

Even *I* don't move. My ears are ringing—my stars Breslin can be loud.

"Sanna?"

I drop my hands from where I'm covering Kota's ears. "Yeah?"

"Are you alright?"

"We're fine. No worries; it just startled me."

"The wagon taking off or my shout?" he ask knowingly.

I chuckle. "Let's just say I wasn't expecting either." I'm quiet for a moment. Breslin's voice sounds like far-off thunder as he murmurs soft commands to the animal he's training. "Will it interrupt you if I ask questions while you work?"

"Not at all. I need to show more than speak at the moment; communication for this part is mostly done with the body. Leg commands and guiding with the rein."

Very cool. "Will Meesahrah be having little Meesahrahs?"

"A terrifying thought."

"Oh please. You make it sound like she's a terror."

"She *is*."

"You'd love her babies." As if she's agreeing with me, Meesahrah chooses this moment to moo.

I can hear Breslin smiling even though I think I detect that his words sound a little bit sad. "Meesahrah hasn't settled with a pair of salkells, and she's a bit advanced in age for breeding; if she hasn't chosen her males by now, she likely never will."

"Wait, girls pick two boys?"

"Salks pick two salkells."

"How... how does that even work?"

"Both keep her company in the manner you'd expect in order for there to result in offspring, but in nature, one salkell is left to raise the offspring while the other salkell and the salk do the hunting. In captivity, fed well in their paddock or no, they still require a trio before they'll breed."

"Sounds complicated."

"Keeps prices driven up; Narwari are tricky to multiply and that works well and fair for me. Unless you want to break a wild Narwari you buy a captive bred one, and not many attempt it. Even fewer are successful. Even so, there are only so many farms that manage to raise offspring."

"Does your farm?"

"When the Creator smiles on me." He clucks to the Narwari he's riding. "Hup, hup. Gooood. Aren't you a treasure? Look how well you're doing."

My lips curve, listening to him. "I've wondered how dog trainers part with their guide dog pupils." My hand finds Kota's neck and I sink my fingers into her ruff. "It's like, how do you manage without getting attached? Well, you'd know: what's your secret?"

"Keep in mind I can't speak for dog trainers..." He murmurs something to the Narwari-in-training before the sound of him sliding off her back reaches my ears. He praises her lavishly and even Kota wags her tail. Even though they aren't aimed at us his affirmations of worthiness feel good. "What's my secret? I *always* get attached. I cut a little bit of my heart away when I send them off."

"That's so sad."

"Ah, that's the nature of the business. The gift is in connecting with great souls, making my living by leaving them a little better than I found them; I'm not meant to keep them."

He moves to his next pupil. "This is the smallest salkell I've ever seen. My heels will touch the ground when I ride him, krit."

"Really?"

"No, but... nearly."

"Does that mean he's too small to do work?"

"Oh he'll do fine; Narwari are strong. A three day old could carry you, and in a season, any weanling could carry me. Smaller does not equate to weaker, not in this species."

Puttering around us is Fellmoor, who's been cleaning Narwari tack while he waits for Breslin's training sessions to end. I ask Fellmoor if I can help, and that's how I end up confirming the source of Breslin's de facto cologne: he smells like Narwari, salty island chips—and

Iechydmaw saddle soap. It seems like we should be eating the paste instead of rubbing it into leather. This stuff smells good enough to lick. While my hands keep busy, Fellmoor is actually nice company, telling interesting stories from when he and Breslin were boys and Breslin was following his father and grandfather out on training Comms.

Supposedly there was a time when Breslin was small—difficult to picture—and because he had nerves of steel and could cling like a... some sort of tree dwelling creature? My translator keeps popping in a mental idea of a person singing—anyway, Breslin was often the first one to ride newly-broke Narwari. Apparently, there were times his job could get rather harrowing.

Fellmoor's stories are so outrageous I'm laughing and Breslin is letting his legend build by not uttering a word of protest which only makes the stories funnier until finally he breaks and belly laughs so loud Kota barks happily.

But then his laughter cuts off abruptly. I wonder why until his hand lands on my lower back and he murmurs, "Hurts?"

It *does* ache but the fact that he noticed? "How...?"

"Look at your nose wrinkle." He laughs under his breath, and I hear what he *doesn't* say: *you're a strange little alien, but I'm fond of you.* "I saw you grimace even as you were attempting to smile," he explains. "You tried to rub right here," he murmurs, one of his knuckles hitting the spot better than I was able to manage. "Is it the seat? It isn't the most forgiving. Do you want to try walking it out?"

"In just a minute," I confirm. "Please don't let me keep you from whatever magic you're working. On me, not the Narwari—you just keep massaging in case that wasn't clear."

"Ha, the Narwari act like they believe it's magic too." He thinks he's making a joke, but I'm not so sure his Narwari are wrong about this ability he has. Some of my muscles loosen like he's ordering them to do it, and when they don't all listen, he digs his thumb and fingers into them until everything submits under his ministrations.

I basically melt into a useless puddle of goo.

"There," he croons, digits giving one last tender massage before he drops his hand. "Let me help you both down and you can stretch your legs a bit before we trek to the homestead."

By the time we leave Fellmoor's farm, none of the weirdness that we came in with remains, and Breslin seems much more relaxed, parting ways with his client/friend in an upbeat mood.

I'm so relieved that I fail to take notice of the little signs my body was trying to give me.

I'M NORMALLY A PREPARED person. But yesterday there was the thing with Fellmoore and Breslin and I got distracted. Then there was Breslin talking to Fellmoor's Narwari and I got *distracted.*

You could say I really like it when Breslin uses his trainer voice—a smooth, low weapon of sound that hypnotizes beasts with an ease rivaled only by how well it works on me. I started asking him questions while he was in work-voice mode just to give myself a thrill.

He was telling me what everyone does to prepare for each of this planet's seasons, what crops need planting or pruning or harvesting. With so much to do and an ever-changing array of tasks, he doesn't have much time to get bored. With my arrival in his life, he's *really* not going to get bored. That becomes obvious about five seconds after we wake up.

Breslin's just rolling out of bed—and we've well established this routine where he gets up, does the bathroom, dressing, and bite-of-breakfast thing and heads for the barn—and on a *normal* day, once I hear him rummaging in the kitchen that's my cue.

I crawl out from under the cooling (formerly Breslin-heated) covers, promise Kota I'll be just a few minutes, and by the time Breslin tells me he'll see me at the barn before he shuts the door behind him, I'll be doing my morning routine in privacy just like I prefer to.

But this morning, when Breslin moves off the bed, he doesn't have to cup my shoulder and ask me if I'm alive—because I'm *awake*. So awake. I'm experiencing that odd snap to consciousness where I go from completely vampire-dead to fully risen and I'm instantly aware of *exactly* why. It's care of my instantly angry uterus who has a blatant disregard for the fact we're stranded on an alien planet where Kotex is not a thing and our temporarily adopted alienman can't make a quick run to the store for us even if he wanted to.

The signs were there: the backache yesterday that came out of nowhere, the tightness in my head—just a light headache but lurking like the warning it was trying to be. I missed it, and I missed my chance to bring this up to Breslin before I started oozing blood on his bed.

It feels like my uterus has been on a complete rampage while I tried to innocently snooze away. Achey, sloppy, bloating; ugh. I'm careful not to shift so as not to upset the fragile balance: I feel a trickle between my legs but this can easily become a red Niagara falls. My voice comes out rusty but alert: "Do you have something that will mop up blood?"

Breslin's voice comes out gravelly and attractively deep—and more alert than even mine. *"Blood?"*

I've got to hand it to this alien, he rolls with anything. He's instantly in action.

"Don't move," he orders. His feet thud softly to the floor. "Where are you bleeding? Why? And why don't you sound alarmed?"

"It's my—"

"Here," he's already back and pressing something soft against my hand.

I feel less awkward in this moment than I have mid-relationship with men on Earth. This alien managed to do a better job carefully shaving my legs with what felt like a machete than I can accomplish with a women's safety razor and that takes trust—that *makes* trust. I can hear him searching for more rags, and as he does, I give him a crash course in the female reproductive system.

He's handing me a towel that I can slide under myself when he clarifies—and by that, I mean exclaims in horror—"Your insides are *shedding?*"

"That's... yeah, that's what they're doing exactly," I confirm. Despite the best efforts of the rag I furtively stuffed between my legs, the second I try to sit up and shift onto the towel, I feel like I soak everything underneath of me. It may even bleed down into the sheet; it *feels* that bad. "Fun conversation: I might have stained your bed just now. I'm so so—"

He doesn't let me finish apologizing. He's entirely matter-of-fact. "Sanna, I grew up on a farm." The tea kettle starts banging on the stove, a precursor to its particularly shrill squeal. It sounds like Breslin carelessly clanks it on a cool burner before he adds, "As long as it's natural and not life-threatening, stop worrying yourself and drink tea."

"Tea?"

"This tea," he presses a cup into my hands. "It helps a little with pain."

So I drink his tea, shuffle to the toilet to clean myself up, and I do stop worrying. Breslin's a natural caregiver. He incorporates the disruption to his morning as if it's simply a task to check off before chores:

Help my bleeding human.

Tackle rest of day.

He doesn't make me feel like my needs are slowing him down even as the Narwari cry outside the door like they're starved to skin and bones in the (maybe) twenty minutes (and counting) it's taking away from their usual breakfast time routine. Right before he leaves, Breslin taps my leg and tells me, "Take all the time you need—and finish your tea. I steeped another cup for you."

After the door closes, I run my fingernail along the side of my thumb. The extra mile of care Breslin just went out of his way to give me, paired with his easygoing practicality the entire time he was doing it... I've just been whalloped with the strongest sense of intimacy I've ever felt with anyone.

Breslin's beyond likable. I almost wish I hadn't had so many hits of his sweetness. He's dangerously addictive.

CHAPTER 16

SANNA

Breslin knocks and asks if I want him to take Kota for a quick walk since it's taking me a bit longer this morning to get ready.

Normally, I'd never consider sending my four-pawed partner off with anyone. Normally, Kota would refuse to move if someone tried. But I hear her move to the door when Breslin mentions her name, and she's a brilliant dog; I think she gets the gist of the conversation just fine. "If she'll go with you, that'd be great. Thank you." I'm so grateful to him. "Kota, do you have to toilet? Will you go with Breslin?"

"She's looking back at you over her withers..." Breslin narrates. "But she's exiting the house. Looks like we're good to try."

"When you get to the spot you want her to go you can say 'get busy' too."

There's definitely a smile in his voice. "I've heard you instruct her with that phrase. I'll be sure to tell her. When you're ready, join us, and if we're successful or not she's at least had the opportunity to relieve herself."

"Sounds good," I confirm as he shuts the door.

A few minutes later, my head is halfway to stuck as I fight to get some type of cable-knit shirt on—yes, yes, I have it right, this is the neck and not a sleeve, goodness it's snug—when there's a loud scratch at the door.

Before I can do more than struggle *harder* to either emerge or escape the garment strangling me like a sweatersquid, the door sounds like it's about to cave in and I hear Breslin: "Easy, easy, I told you I'd let you in; just give me a moment—"

The sound of the handle seems to reach my ears at the same time Kota lands on me. Squeal-whining, she proceeds to fill me in on her adventure, her tail beating at me as she wags it wildly. Thankfully, her initial bump into me helped my head break free of the sweaterneck canal and I'm officially wearing this thing.

I may not be able to get *out* of it, but by God, I've got it on.

"Hey, Kota," I hug her hard and one of her paws comes up over my arm and clings like she's hugging me back. "Were you good?"

"She used the outdoor facilities," Breslin confirms. "Do you need any assistance?"

Feeling shy, I squeeze Kota for a second as I say, "Nope, but thanks. What's on the itinerary for today?"

"Once the Narwari are fed, it's time to travel to another appointment, this one for trimming more than training. Care to join me?"

I do. And that's how weeks go by. Breslin makes the time pass so easily and despite the routine not deviating much, somehow our time together is never boring, nothing gets stale.

In everything he does, it's obvious Breslin's trying his best to make my time here as comfortable and pleasant as possible, and his efforts have been appreciated—but the thing that keeps me from falling into more than the occasional bout of homesickness is him.

It's Breslin.

He makes me feel so... accepted. I'm not 'the blind girl.' I'm Sanna.

Sometimes, I feel so content that I wonder if maybe I miss the *idea* of home more than I actually miss it. But then I think of my family. My mom. My dad. My zany sister. Their kennel where I love to go when there's a litter of roly poly puppies. The thought of being separated from them by more than mere miles makes my chest actually ache. At least I have Kota. Technically, we've been going it on our own for a while and although I can survive without day to day contact from loved ones—Kota is the exception. I'd go crazy if she wasn't with me.

But no matter how much I'm missing home, Breslin's always there, making me happy to be with him even if *here* is not where I chose to be.

Case in point: my day's been sailing along, chipper and bright, all because it started with Breslin squeezing my toes where I was cocooned in the blankets as he left the house. That tiny scrap of contact has had me smiling and humming even though we're under a bit of a time crunch: today is another training-and-hoof trimming, but this farm is even farther out than the others so we need to book it as soon as we finish feeding the Narwari pack.

The buckets are barely done being stacked but I can feel Kota's anticipation. She *loves* wagon rides. Honestly? So do I.

Unlike me though, when we get to the wagon, Kota eagerly scrambles into it, effortlessly making the leap up from a standstill. I beam a smile up in her direction. Breslin cheers for her job well done and sets off the percussion of her tail against the benchseat's back.

I cheer too because this is a seriously impressive jump. I sure can't make it. Luckily, I don't have to. Breslin's hands land on my hips, and he gives me the lift I need. And not gonna lie: having Breslin's hands on me is my secret highlight to these trips. To think that being lifted up and down from the wagon used to make me nervous. *Not anymore.*

"What has you smiling like this?" Breslin asks as he joins me.

"Just having a happy morning," I tell him.

"At least it'll get me good tips," he mutters.

When he doesn't say anything more, I make a noise of protest. "WHAT did you just say? You can't just drop something like that and not explain!"

Breslin bumps me as he shifts his immense form on the unforgiving wooden seat. "I've worked the trainer and farrier circuit my whole life."

"Alright."

"And I've gotten my fair share of tips for jobs well done."

"Okay."

"But all of a sudden every farmer has blessed us with a fat gift on top of the amount due. Prichard's gratuity being the biggest. I'm convinced it's your smile that's doing it."

An astonished laugh startles out of me.

To this Breslin only says, "And *that*. Creator help them if they ever hear you laugh."

Feeling a little tongue-tied, I don't say anything for a beat. I'm surprised Prichard gave us anything extra at all—he seemed so *grumpy*. Breslin had claimed that the other alien is normally lighthearted and would be back to his normal self by the next time we saw him, but it'd been kind of hard to imagine.

Other than him, everyone else *has* gone out of their way to be friendly and keep me entertained—in the literal, old-fashioned sense: funny stories, a temperature-appropriate drink and sweetened snacks. At first, I'd been nervous at all the attention, but it was the polite kind, and Breslin told me I was the only female for 'sticks and sticks,' so I should expect to be pampered.

I've found out it's kinda nice to be pampered. I also like being protected—which is good, because Breslin acts just a tiny bit, exhilaratingly possessive. He doesn't let anyone stand in my personal space, he doesn't let the chatting go on too long or get too personal and I've received the impression that these males are all a little bit intimidated by Breslin.

It never fails to feel good. I love training and hoof trimming days. Still, I'm stunned. A smile from a woman makes these lonely aliens *tip* us better? A *smile?* Finally I manage, "You're serious."

"As a hobbled Narwari."

I snort. "A *hobbled* Narwari—would that be another way of saying you're homicidal with indignation?"

"Very near."

Not sure how I should take this, but feeling my insides flutter with a thrill, I clear my throat and I pose a nice, safe question. "What are we doing with these tips?"

I hear a scuffing sound I associate with Breslin when he's in his thinking mode. I still don't know what it comes from but I'm finally comfortable enough with him that I reach up and touch his face—taking him by surprise—and find he's got his fingers on his jaw.

I give him an impersonal feel-up; searching all around the length of his jaw, the bottom of his chin, the base of his throat, trying to find stubble or hairs or some reason he itches and what makes the noise when he does it.

I don't find anything. "I give. What makes the noise?"

"This?" he wiggles his fingers under mine, and I hear the scuffing again.

I catch and turn over his fingers and it's his *skin*—his finger pads and the skin on his face is just rough enough to make this light scraping sound when the surfaces press together.

"While you're there you may as well make your little nails useful. Give me a scratch, would you?"

I snort on him, but I do as he asks, giving him a little scritch before I plop back down, my hands dropping to my lap. "Mystery solved."

"That's it?" Breslin asks. "You were doing so well, and I wasn't done."

I laugh and raise up on my knees and anchor myself on his shoulder to give him another go. I laugh harder when he arches his neck for me just like one of his Narwari so that I can get all of his itchy spots.

His voice is a grateful, vibrating groan when he declares, "Done well, Sanna. Plenty thanks."

I drop down beside him again and take hold of my original question. "You were in the middle of answering me."

"Was I?"

I pretend to nod primly. "You were. You were about to reveal what we're doing with the scads of money I'm earning my master."

He nudges me, and it's a small movement for him, but I have to catch myself so I don't slide across the bench. Breslin helps by tugging me back to his side, and even though his voice is gruff, he pats my leg softly. "Disrespectful little creature. I thought you might like to go to dinner in town."

I clap my hands together. "Oooh, I'd like that. Alien restaurants!"

"Hold onto that smile, *alien,* and we'll be able to *buy* the restaurants."

I grin up at him and he mutters to himself and my happy feelings stay as we roll on to the next unsuspecting farm.

And when he finishes up the job and packs us back into the wagon, Breslin presses a drawstring bag into my lap, his fingers brushing my thighs and, despite his touch being incidental and delivered in an impersonal way, it still has my thighs clenching. "Your share of the scads."

I hug the heavy bag to me all the way to the little one-room farmhouse.

CHAPTER 17

SANNA

Slowly, I come to that awareness where my body is so relaxed I'm boneless but my neck is stretched to the point it makes swallowing too awkward to keep sleeping through. It's choke to death or wake up, and doggone it, no matter how much I love sleep, consciousness is winning by seeping increments. Mostly because every attempt to swallow makes my head reflexively snap back, like a baby bird when you try to spoon food down it's gullet. My neck is stretched because my face is not pillowed, my face is not cushioned—my face is propped up too high on what should not feel so darn good: an unforgivingly hard-muscled bicep.

I gurgle in satisfaction and don't strain myself to get up. This is too nice, and there are worse things than a stiff neck.

Judging by the length of pipe branding the back of my thigh, Breslin would agree there are many *stiff* things worse off than my neck.

"Are you awake?" Breslin asks in a rumbly purr that has me wanting to stretch and climb on top of him.

"Mmhmm," I manage to mumble back. If I wiggle down and press myself to him in invitation, would he be receptive?

I'm Breslin-infatuated. I'm crazy for his voice, his smell, and his hands on me. He's made me an addict when it comes to sleeping with him. But I want more than actual sleeping. I want to do all the things in this bed that have *nothing* to do with sleeping. I hope he's as worked up about me as I am about him—yes he's hard at the moment, but that could be anything. Penises do things, all sorts of things.

Just as I'm making the decision to be bold and either outright ask him or outright jump him, he slides out of bed, taking his pillowing arm with him.

Noooo...

The sounds of him getting ready for the day are nice ones though, so I lie in a heap of sexual fever and listen to him going through his usual routine. It's a sweet sort of torture. I groan and turn over, grimacing when my thighs rub together and it feels both better and leaves me feeling even more alone. I've never had a roommate. Maybe this sexual desire and crazy sexual tension develops for every roommate situation and most individuals just politely go about ignoring it.

I don't think I have the skill. Not where Breslin's concerned. How would I even go about building up such a resistance? I listen to him whistle as he dresses, smell his sharp, musky pillow as it cools next to my head, and feel his hand squeeze my foot over the blankets as he tells me he'll see me in the far pasture, or in the stalls or wherever he'll be as he works up his (*really really excellent smelling*) sweat for the day.

I bear it all and I *don't* proposition him. I have the self control muscles of Chris Hemsworth-as-Thor proportions, clearly.

"Will you come see me soon?" he asks me, and it's the playfulness in his tone that makes my toes curl. Plus, he's still holding my foot in his hand and it's doing all sorts of things—his touch is traveling right up my leg like a clear highway to my welcome center station and I cannot concentrate on anything else.

That's why I answer with a drugged and dreamy, "*Uh huh.*"

He squeezes my toes again and my thighs jump. This man breaks animals for a living and my good gravy I believe he does it well. The word *breaking* used to conjure a painful connotation in my mind but in this moment, I believe with the fervor of a thousand swooning hearts that Breslin doesn't have to beat or terrorize any of his conquests. Softly spoken commands and gentle whispering touches from him would have me twitching and writhing and begging him to tell me what to do in about five seconds flat.

"Good salk," he says softly—YES! Softly, damn him!—and I reexamine my five seconds time frame. Maybe nanoseconds would be more honest.

Man I'm going to miss Breslin like crazy when I go home.

It's a thought that's been weighing heavily on my mind. Breslin-like men do not grow on trees. I'm not even sure they exist—I mean, sure, they might but what's that saying? What do good men, hard-working men, and wonderful men have in common? *They're already married.*

Soon, we'll be separated by more than the still largely incomprehensible measure of 'sticks'—we're going to be separated by *galaxies.* Just the thought makes me miss him.

If I go home, I'll never get to enjoy all the wonder that is Breslin again.

My throat closes.

When Breslin gathers his breakfast and announces that the house is all mine to get ready for the day in private, I wait just long enough for him to close the door before I roll over and use my spare moments of privacy to cry into my pillow. Kota's tags jingle and the bed depresses as she puts her paws near my shoulder, and laying her head close enough to my face that she can touch me with her nose. She whimpers and I sob into alien goose feathers—or whatever fluffy things plump the pillows—as I remind myself of all the reasons it's worth going back home.

CHAPTER 18

SANNA

Breslin's in the barn, tinkering on one of his wagons, a flatbed that has no canvas top. Kota and I nearly baked in the sun when we rode in it yesterday so he's adding a shade over the seat.

It's so thoughtful that when he informed me of what he was doing, I think I managed to mumble a shaky "Oh! Thanks," a second ahead of giving Kota the forward command where I hightailed it outside before I could do something embarrassing. Like throw myself on him.

Normally, I keep him company when he's working but it's been getting harder and harder not to clamp onto him and forget all the reasons I'd miss home if I stayed.

It's getting harder and harder to believe that once I'm home, I won't miss Breslin more than I ever missed Earth.

Kota wuffs and I know we must be approaching Meesahrah. This is her special greeting for the odd Narwari. We're walking along the inside rail of the fenceline in the main pasture, and we've gone quite a ways out. I think best when I'm walking and I walk a lot when I'm thinking. Breslin told me we're plenty safe if I want to pace like this. He says there aren't predators in the area, not anymore, and certainly nothing left that would be fool enough to take on a Narwari. So Kota and I pace in the safety of Breslin's pack of alien meat-eating horses. They may not be demonstrative, cuddly animals but they like having us join them. If they didn't, I think we'd be eaten already.

To reset myself, I sing. Just softly at first, but I hear more and more Narwari hooves join us. They sound like they're flocking to us. Just for the music, I'm sure, and not a 'dinner and a show' type deal, ha ha. Sometimes, they still manage to make me a tiny bit nervous, though they've been incredibly conscientious so far. It's really only when I hear them cracking bones from whatever Breslin's fed them that morning. I switch songs and finally, I feel light enough that when I hear Kota panting up at me, I can smile back at her.

But the harness handle I'm gripping abruptly stops moving forward—and so do I. Kota's come to a halt for some reason.

"What is it?" I ask her, reaching my arm up in front of me. One of the most difficult concepts to teach Kota was something all guide dogs are trained to do: pay such close attention to their surroundings, they notice when something is hanging down and could wonk you upside the head—like the tree branch my hand just encountered. "Perfect alert, way to go, sal—"

I almost said 'salk.' I smile sadly. *Breslin's influence.* "Good girl! Good job."

I pick up the song I was singing at the refrain, adjust my grip on Kota's harness, and—

Something drops from the tree and latches onto my shoulder.

Kota goes *wild.*

All I can feel is its weight and its claws and as I instinctively try to block my face, it clutches onto me tighter, chittering.

Surely this creature isn't fool enough to take on a Narwari! Although, it didn't take on a Narwari, did it? But Breslin said any predators are long gone, hunted to extinction by Narwari packs. *What would be the odds that something came back?* I don't know, but my heart's racing and I wish Breslin were here.

Kota's teeth snap and the creature squeals and it launches itself off of my shoulder and scrambles back into the tree.

"Okay," I pant, trying to take stock. I felt claws, but I don't think it pierced through my clothing. I don't feel like I'm bleeding anywhere. I don't think it bit me without me noticing.

Kota leans against me like, *Whew! What was THAT?* Her tail wags against my leg once.

"Allll right," I breathe. "That was kind of a lot more exciting than I expected this walk to be. Let's head back and have a little chat with Breslin." I duck for the low branch, and pick up the song I was working on with almost a desperate sort of cheerfulness. *I'm not afraid of the unknown arboreal alien.*

Kota goes tense beside me again.

A dried leaf crackles and I *know* the thing is right above me. Waiting.

It drops on me.

Kota lets out an indignant roar and lunges—

I nearly collapse from the force with which the creature uses my shoulder as a springboard to return to the safety of the branches.

We scurry away from the stand of trees, heading at a brisk, brisk pace—and for one of Kota's breed, this is really saying something. Kota whines all the way back to the barn and in the manner that only a German shepherd can—a series of sharp, whistling mumbles as she—at great, *loud* length—discusses her feelings on the matter of this pasture interloper.

"San San? What's amiss?" Breslin calls, his deep voice carrying great, but it still takes several minutes before I make it the distance it takes so that he can hear *me*.

One of us, but my money's on Kota, is acting shaken enough that when I relay my description of our alien encounter, Breslin drops whatever he's working on and asks us to lead him to the trees we were under.

As we approach the copse of trees where the mystery animal dropped on us, Kota nearly makes *words* with her whines she gets so excited—clearly, she knows Breslin's here to sort this out and she wants it done right. She feels we were under a grievous attack, and being the great guy he is, Breslin doesn't hesitate to be brave and mighty. He shimmies right up the tree we stop at.

"Do you often climb the trees?" I ask.

He huffs, "Tevek no, I haven't climbed since I was a boy."

"How is it?"

"High."

I snicker.

"It's a bit of a shame though, who'd have thought? Life experience has sucked the thrill out of this whole tree scaling experience."

"Why do you say that?"

"Because I've learned falling hurts."

I half-gasp, half chortle. "Remember when you told me *'That's what everybody says at first?'*"

"Salk, when it comes to falling out of a kritted tree, believe me it's the *last* thing you say too."

I smother a laugh. Kota bumps my leg, and I rub her ear. To Breslin, I call, "Do you see anything?"

He inhales the sweet smelling air. "I see so much from up here. No creature, but crite this farm is nice."

The awed pride in his voice has me smiling.

"Well," he says, a little strain to his words as he starts to carefully move down the tree, "Let's hope it's something that isn't too dangerous."

"Yeah," I agree mildly. "Not *too* dangerous."

He chuffs a laugh. "Allow me to rephrase. Let's hope it's curious but not unkind."

THE NEXT MORNING, BRESLIN'S chopping up a downed tree for firewood. He tosses the chopped chunks to the side, and very slowly, very carefully, I collect the hunks and carry them one by one to the waiting flatbed wagon.

I'm humming to myself as I dust off my hands and holler, "I have to take a pee break!" to Breslin.

"My back is to you," he responds, adding, "There's wipe clothes on the wagon seat."

Ah, wipe clothes. I miss disposable toilet paper. Rags—soft ones, but still rags—are what's used here to clean up after relieving oneself. It's quite the process: used rags get soaked in a bucket of cleaning solution, churned with a stick, rinsed, wrung, hung to dry, and collected as the next batch of rear-end wipes.

I really, *really* miss toilet paper.

When the sounds of rhythmic chopping are pretty muted, I find a tree, for no other reason than it feels more secure to pee behind something than it does to drop down in the open, and grab my pants.

This set has a row of buttons. I haven't had to work buttons on my clothes since I was a child. It's zippers and velcro for everything now—or it was. My humming switches to chanting as I fumble them all free. By the time I finally get to the part where I'm relieving myself, well? I'm feeling serious relief, and I sing it out.

Kota goes tense just as I'm starting to stand back up. I scream when something grabs my hair.

Breslin bellows, *"Sanna?"*

Small clawed hands and feet grip along my shoulders and Kota sounds like she's about to explode. I don't have to speak dog to know what she's freaking out about.

It's the thing! The thing is back!

Boots pound across the pasture but Breslin's too late; by the time he reaches us, it's just me and a turbulently talkative Kota.

"Tree visitor," I say by way of explanation.

He's a little winded, but he pats my shoulders—not to reassure me, not *just* to reassure me, but to make sure I'm unhurt. "It found you again? Well I'll be kritted. Wait, what were you doing?"

"Doing?" *Peeing?* "Nothing! It just dropped on me."

Breslin's fingers brush against mine, making my brain trip. And I think: *I should be applying hand sanitizer before we touch.* And then I think *People lick each other's* genitals: *if Breslin wants to touch my* hand *before I wash it, we'll live.* My thoughts have veered so, so very far off that it takes me a second to process what he's saying. "No, you were doing something and doing it well. What was it?"

I start to stammer, "Oh, I was sing—" but I register his words. *And doing it well.* "I really don't—"

"You were singing?" he prompts—but then he does something so mind-blowing, I don't know how he expects me to be able to answer. His hands grasp either side of my pants, which made it over my hips but I never got them refastened.

One by one, Breslin quietly feeds the button rounds through the slits and instead of making me feel incapable of putting on my own pants, Breslin's soft touch makes me feel cared for. And as he strokes his fingers along the sides of my hips, dragging his touch over me just a little, my insides basically combust. My internal temperature skyrockets to a balmy nine thousand degrees, melting my brain completely.

So completely that when Breslin rumbles, "Sing for me," I nearly choke on my tongue trying. I pull through, but he's managed to unintentionally work me into such a fluttery state, I'm a stanza in before I stumble to silence—though I don't pull out of his hands.

Because something is touching my shoulder.

I jump when a length of fluff slithers over me and wraps around my neck. *Please be a tail, please be a tail—a super cute tail, nothing scary.*

Kota isn't even breathing she's gone so still. Apparently Breslin's presence makes her feel like she doesn't need to defend my safety; kind of nice really. A sign she super trusts him.

Evidently I do too, because I place my hands over his as I feel four small fingers with four long claws touch down.

Kota stiffens but doesn't bark.

The thing eases all four feet onto me, giving me all of its weight and I don't move. But I do flinch when a crunch happens right next to my ear. "Ah!"

"S'alriiight," Breslin soothes.

Kota wuffs in warning.

The animal crunches again and I feel little dry crumbs sprinkle my clothing and some goes right down the neck of my shirt. Ick. I hope it's munching on an alien version of a walnut or something and not like the shell of a bug.

"This is a yushabee," Breslin murmurs. "I've only seen the captive bred ones in the city. They were rounded up here until we thought they were gone."

"Oh yeah? I don't think this yushabee got the memo. It feels very, very present and right here and *not* in captivity in the city."

"What's a memo?"

Breslin's question is so serious but still delivered in that calming tone that I shudder as I try not to laugh—I'm afraid of upsetting this yushabee.

The urge to laugh dies an instant death the moment Breslin's fingers smooth up my side, over my ribs, headed for the yushabee but my body does not know this or it doesn't care. My body is offering up all sorts of suggestions for what Breslin should do next and where else he should roam his hand when he whispers, "You have to sing very, very skillfully to draw them out."

I digest this. "What does it look like?"

There's a sound like Breslin pops his tongue against the roof of his mouth. "It's got more fur than you and Kota combined. Very plush."

"Cuddly?"

"What?"

"Like it makes someone want to hug it?"

There's a brief beat of silence. "It's possible." His tone says a whole lot more, like, *only if you wanted to get bitten.*

Scary.

"It has large ears, sort of shaped like your Kota but... more rounded at the outer edges."

"Sounds like a bat," I offer.

"I'll take your word for it. It's got a long tail, the fur is even longer there. The way it's sitting, its back is arched so it looks like a giant ball of fluff with ears. And eyes."

"It has big eyes?"

"Huge."

What an odd mental picture. "Cute ones?"

There's a longer pause than before. "If you like that sort of... I suppose. In a way..." he trails off and I smile at his earnestness as he examines the animal. "It's mouth is almost nonexistent—which is ironic—barely a bump on its face with tiny lips under a button nose."

"Why is a small mouth ironic?"

"You should see the... nevermind. It's feet—"

I'm on alert. "What should—or shouldn't—I see? What is it?"

"Its teeth," Breslin says reluctantly.

"They're huge too?" I say weakly.

The animal crunches on whatever it's eating again and it's a disturbingly loud sound. I think I even hear the slice of teeth. I mean, I'm pretty sure.

"You don't want to know," Breslin says finally. "In the city, they use them to teach children vocal control. When the yushabee hears a note that falls out of pitch, they bite."

The grip of the yushabee's toes instantly takes on a sinister feel and my shoulder starts to sink under the animal's slight weight.

But Breslin's hand catches my upper arm. He laughs quietly, but heartily. It makes my insides shiver like a happy tuning fork. "You're in no danger. They give these to children: the bite can't be too serious."

"Too serious!" I exclaim even as Breslin's musing, "Although, come to think of it, a lot of opera stars wear masquerade masks. I always assumed it was for mystery. Huh."

Not even daring to breathe, I squeak, "Are you joshing again?"

"Not this time."

I whisper-yelp, "Breslin get it off of me, get it off!"

He makes this sound, this punch of sound peculiar to him and I think it originates in his throat but it definitely puffs out of his nose and it is an *amused* noise. "All right, let me see if it will come to me—"

The yushabee springs off my shoulder.

"Do you have it?" I ask, feeling a little panicked at the thought of a face-eating creature lunging for Breslin.

"It went back up into the tree. Crite, they can really jump. I want to hear you sing again."

"You let it GO? And *what?!* You want me to lure it back? No!"

His hands take hold of my shoulders, and just like that, my horror evaporates. He's got serious skills with these little touches. He also has serious skills with sweet words. "I want to hear you sing, because I want to hear you sing. We can do it inside if you'd feel better."

My brain's sexual switch is tripped hard. I'm imagining just what we could do inside and how it would make me feel better.

Lots and lots and lots better.

"Sanna?"

"Hmm?"

One big hand abandons the tender hold he had on my shoulder, making it want to cry. But then my whole back whooshes hot as he fits his hand at the magnetizing spot just barely above my butt. Whenever he touches me here, I swear my brain shuts right off and my entire concentration is focused on the heat, the size, and the feel of his hand. However, my brain proves it does *not* shut off entirely, because it starts supplying suggestions of what else his hand could be doing.

"Do you want to do it inside with me?"

Ohhh do I ever. "Yes." I nod emphatically. "This is a brilliant idea. We should do this inside. Together."

Breslin uses only my above-butt pressure point to get me turned and guide me into falling into step next to him. My hip rubs against his thigh as we walk and the heat of his body sears me from my shoulder to my calf and I'm imagining all the things I want to do inside with him, yes, yes, yes. *A lot.* We could do it on the bed. Against the wall. Against the door. On the floor. In the rain. On a train—

"—he's not going to wait. What do you say?"

I blink a few times and try to clear the positions out of my head. "I'm sorry. I was... daydreaming."

"Of what?"

"What?" *No, don't ask me that!* "Who's not going to wait?"

Breslin hooks his whole arm around my back and I suck in a happy breath but he only tugs me so that my shoulder bumps into him—an affectionate little squeeze—and then he takes his limb back.

Goosebumps have broken out all over my body and I'm so lightheaded I could drop right here.

If I do, he might carry me.

OKAY!

"Darrow wants his Narwari's hooves trimmed and he needs them done before harvest starts. It's a good thing he's got a solid reason, otherwise, I'd be convinced he's just fishing."

Darrow is a really nice guy. He uses the word *'moonringed'* when referring to me—he uses it a lot—and it's sweet. It's always paired with the nicest compliments. "For what?"

"To see you again."

I stop walking. "Why?"

Breslin's arm does the slide-and-grip-squeeze again and I just about melt. I'm convinced that if he gives me a couple more good squeezes like this I'll come.

"Because he's attracted to you," Breslin answers, putting pressure to his spot on my back to start me walking again and I can't tell if it's just wishful thinking, or if he actually sounds a little nettled about this.

"Darrow? Are you sure? How can you tell?"

"Sanna," Breslin says, and squeezes me again—

Just like that! Harder! Harder! Don't stop!

Kota bumps my leg and I shake my head to clear it.

"His dijjü had filled up and were showing dark the last time we were there."

"Dijjü... that's those things... on your head?"

"That's right. His body is priming visual receptors for a potential lifemate. He can't hide his interest in you."

The words leave my mouth before I can clamp down on them. "Do yours swell... dark?"

Breslin's hand leaves my back, taking his warmth, his hardness, and his mind-blowing touch away as we reach the wagon and he moves off to retrieve his axe. "Of late? All the time."

CHAPTER 19

SANNA

Did he mean that his dijjü swell in general? Or are his dijjü swelling for me as his—*his potential lifemate?*

It doesn't seem like the translation could get clearer. Breslin's not looking for an I'm-stranded-for-now, we-like-each-other, let's-have-fun fling. He wants more. So do I.

But I'd have to give up everything.

That's all. Just everything.

Breslin's going to kill me and it'll be accidental on his part but I'll be dead all the same. Because I want it all: I want him, *and* I want my home—I want everything, I want it all so much it hurts.

We're in bed, and I can feel warm patches on me where the sunlight is pouring in through the windows. Breslin's slept late and I know this because he's sprawled on top of me.

I love it.

I'd love it more if he wasn't dead asleep.

I want to wiggle backward and find out if he's hard this morning, but I don't.

My self control is honestly astounding. It's also draining, and this is what's going to be the death of me. Every time Breslin hugs me tighter in his sleep, tugs me closer, tucks his chin harder against my neck or half-nuzzles into my hair...

I want to turn in his arms and attack him with my mouth, with my hands—with my starving vagina.

He's really making the celibacy choice painful.

His breathing changes—his chest bows out with his inhale, shoving me deeper into the mattress and my back arches in response and YES he *is* hard and it's sublime.

When he growls to clear his throat, my eyes roll back in my head.

"Good rising, Sanna."

I can't even talk to him. He has no idea that if I open my mouth, I will beg him for things. Mostly filthy, filthy things.

But I also want to beg him for things he can't give me. Like him. Coming home with me. How can I even think to ask him to do the very thing I'm struggling with—walking away from everything he's ever known? The kicker is, his people have been nothing but welcoming to me—warmly so, the alien in their midst.

Earth isn't going to be like this.

Earth's pretty much going to be the exact opposite of this.

To be together, I'd need to be the one to make the sacrifice because Breslin can't do it for me.

I think he would. If Earth wouldn't totally freak out about his arrival, exotic animals have a market and he could make a killing selling predator horses—who wouldn't want to try them out? He'd be like a celebrity alien-equine trainer and we'd live happily ever after on some acreage far away from sheep and cattle farms. (Because yeah, okay—we'd have to find a place where animals won't break into the Narwari's fences and accidentally get themselves drawn in and eaten.)

It's basically a Disney princess story in the making.

I sigh, and Breslin sleepily nuzzles right across my nape. For as heavy as thoughts are weighing on my mind, my body is aware of two things: it has needs, and the alien it wants to satisfy its needs with is, for all intents and purposes, pinning us to the bed.

My body has given all horizontal action from here on out a green light. Chemicals and hormones are being dumped throughout my system, threatening to shut down my thinking brain and just go wild doing the fun thing.

Unaware of my turmoil, Breslin peels himself off of my back, and I want to cry.

Here this alien just wants to get up and go about his busy work day. He'll train his animals to ride and he'll do it without breaking a sweat, while I on the other hand want to stay in bed and get very sweaty riding *him* all day.

His hand lands over my blanket-swaddled hip and I brace myself because he's always sweet-touching me—cute little touches that for him seem to be nothing more than genuine displays of affection, but to me, they turn me into a raging lust beast with a voracious appetite for a Garthmaw.

Affectionately, (always affectionately—*why does he have to be so nice? Why?* This alien deserves affection in return and I want to be the one to slather it on him. *How am I supposed to fight how I feel for him when he's so dang appealing all the dang time?*) he asks, "You coming with me today?"

I bite my cheeks until I can control myself. Breslin's got his sexy-rough sleep voice on and he's asking me if I want to come with him? *Only in all the ways.* "I'll follow in a bit."

His hand slides three and a half inches—I can tell you exactly because I've never been more attuned to a touch on my body in my entire life—and he pats me.

It's like light taps to the cushioned parts of my backside.

Breslin's basically spanking my ass.

He. Is. Killing! Me!

"I look forward to you coming—"

ME TOO: LET'S DO THIS! RIGHT NOW IS GOOD. SO GOOD.

"—along with me today. We could make a day of it after the trimming if you want. Have a meal in town. Sound good?"

"Sounds so good," I manage.

Breslin spanks my ass again in his completely oblivious way and I bury my face into my pillow and bite it.

The sound of him dressing this morning is not nice: it's pure torture and when he finally leaves for chores, he braces himself over me, and I feel the mattress depress on either side of my head and my imagination imagines a very different reason for this. I reach out and feel around until I confirm that he's balancing on his knuckles as he hangs over me. There may or may not be a flutter happening on my insides as a direct result to this data. Ditto for the flutter when my thumbs brush his bulging arms.

His lips touch the top of my head.

The aching spot between my legs clenches so hard, I choke on a whimper.

He pulls back a little. "Are you alright?"

NOPE. I AM NOT. "Umm hmm. I'm great. I'll follow you out in a bit."

The moment the door shuts behind him, I don't wait to politely make sure he didn't forget anything. I roll to my stomach, shove my hand into my panties and come twice without any effort and not nearly as much relief as I need. I reach around for a pillow and cram it against my pelvis and hump out a third orgasm, and finally, I can think again. I desperately try to make that thinking be about something *other* than incredible sex with Breslin, though admittedly, I don't manage my goals well.

A voice booms through the walls, startling me and making Kota clamber to her feet with a clatter of nails on wooden floor boards.

"LAZY SALK!" Breslin's all cheery good nature. "COME, COME."

There's a command I fully endorse. My inner muscles still twitching, I'm unthinkingly making my way off the bed, fitting Kota's harness on, and heading in the direction of Breslin's voice before I've so much as gone to the bathroom or put on a fresh set of clothes.

This alien has me tied in knots and he's not even trying. I wasn't sex starved when I left home. Breslin with his alien-siren self, all hotness and rock-like body, he's melting my brain. Actually, he's turning me into a zombie who isn't moaning for brains—just sex. Lots and lots of sex.

And Breslin. I'm starting to mindlessly want Breslin.

CHAPTER 20

BRESLIN

I pull another hair from my mouth. This human female sheds *terribly*. I find them in my food, curled up in the sink drain, sticking in our bedding, and clinging to the wash basin even after I wipe it dry and hang it on the wall to keep it out of the way. So it should be no surprise when I raise the brush I'm using to gather Sanna's hair for plaiting and find the bristles gummed up beyond reason. Nevermind that it's been sent through only a handful of pulls of her lively mass. "Your shedding problem is rivaled only by your pet's," I say under the pretense of grousing.

With unerring ease, she snatches the brush from my hands and feigns indignation. "You're just jealous because we *have* hair."

I smirk down at her as I go back to weaving hers into the decorative little braids she taught me how to make. I find them fetching.

"Even your Narwari don't have hair," she continues, sounding less teasing and somewhat stymied by this.

"They do too," I counter.

"Where?"

"Their tails," I say, even while I admit to myself that this claim is a bit of a stretch.

"I've owned brooms with softer bristles, you're a liar—that's *not* hair," she finishes in one breath before her voice turns serious, "Sweeping will cut down on the loose hair floating everywhere." Sanna's fingers close over my forearm. "I can't believe I didn't think to ask you for one until now. I'll absolutely sweep up if you have a broom."

My gaze zeroes in on our connection. She finds it incredible that men will toss extra coins in the payment bag just because a pretty salk smiles at them. But Sanna has a way of making a man feel good. Here she is trying to talk about household chores and just this smallest contact of her hand on my arm makes me want to roll her to her back.

Instead, I growl, "Hold still," and finish her last braid before I lose my sense and tackle her to the bed.

Unaware, she continues to argue with me because she loves to engage in battles of words, which is what all of our discussions seem to end in. "But let me guess: if you have a broom, it really *is* made of Narwari tails, isn't it?" She raises her brows, and I watch as one out distances the other. "Is it made of Meesahrah? You're always threatening that poor salk."

I shake off the hunger for her that I sometimes wonder if she's completely unaware of. I'd make my interest plain if I thought Sanna would consider me for her lifemate, but from the beginning, she's made her intention to return home nothing but clear.

I respect that. Somehow, I have to *accept* that. There will come a day when I have to say goodbye. I can feel my dread for that day building every second I breathe her scent, feel her warm softness brush me at night, and every moment we spend apart. It shouldn't be this difficult: after all, aren't I used to being temporary?

I click my teeth, clearing my head and getting into the game. I have to clear my throat twice before I can manage it. "'Poor salk? Poor *salk?*' Bah. The contents of the broom's bristles are—"

From a plant, actually.

"—nothing I'm going to confirm for you."

"Ha! I knew it!" she caws.

Kota's gaze roves from one of us to the other, assessing our moods and deciding I'm not about to attack and consume her mistress or any of the things this animal used to worry about when we first met.

I nod to her. Securing one's trust is done in much the same fashion as one builds a steadfast rampart: brick by brick—and she's really come far where I'm concerned.

Absently, I start to scoop up the odds and ends of human mane care things Sanna's helped me collect for her. I'm caught up in Sanna's scent and the happiness she makes me feel and my tense disquiet for the day she'll be gone so that when her silk-skinned hand catches my arm, without thinking, I catch it back, and drop over her on the bed, pinning her body in place.

"I can put it all away," she says a bit breathlessly. "You shouldn't have to do all the chores around here. Especially when it's my mess. And Breslin, I can *do* this."

What she means is 'let me do something.'

Oh San San. If you only knew what I wish you would do...

You can't keep her. She wants to return home.

I struggle with myself but in the end, I let her up and offer a brisk, "Let's have this dinner we keep threatening each other with." I've been saying she'll charm everyone in the place, and she jests that if that happens (and the men keep throwing money at her as they do) she'll be able to afford to buy up all the alien realestate and she'll roll around town in a *'pihmmp*wagon' with wheels made of gold.

Which is outrageous. Gold is too soft to make a wheel you can rely on.

When I pointed that out, she just laughed and laughed, and I knew that if we'd been sitting in a restaurant just then, that her jest of becoming kritted rich could be halfway to a reality. Her laugh is addictive and awe-inducing. Perhaps it's simply the effect of her being a human, and it's an ability her race possesses.

Or perhaps it's just my Sanna.

"I'd love to go to dinner with you," she says softly, all trace of teasing gone.

And crite, the way she's nibbles on her bottom lip is almost more dangerous than her smile and her laugh combined. I don't know what she's mulling over, but this look she's wearing now—it has me wanting to draw her into my arms.

But I don't. I turn away to get ready to take her out for a night of revelry.

I know our time together is on a backwards count according to whatever the Na'rith's timetable is for their Earthen voyage. All of the moments I have left with Sanna, I want spent well. It doesn't seem possible, but I'm terribly attached to her already, and I'm going to miss her fiercely when she leaves me.

CHAPTER 21

SANNA

Going to the restaurant is different. First off, Breslin examines Ekan's clothes options with quiet deliberation, and then he spends quite a bit of time digging through a wooden box. He sets it just in front of my knees and when I put my hands inside with him, I feel all sorts of things—some of which feels like jewelry. I examine what I think might be a chunky-styled necklace. A pair of heavy rings.

Breslin murmurs in approval when I lift a slightly smaller necklace with oddly carved dangling pieces. "That was my grandmother's. It's made of Narwari bone."

I'm ready to drop it but he laughs and closes my hand tighter over it instead. "The Narwari this ivory was harvested from had already passed away. It was her favorite mount, and she wanted something more to remember him by. A good number of the salks on this farm trace back to him."

"That's kind of cool," I finally say, meaning it.

"May I put it on you?"

I guess an ivory necklace isn't weird. At least this was humanely, legally harvested. "All right."

I bend my neck and his slightly rough-skinned arms brush past my cheeks before I feel his touch at my nape, rolling the clasp tightly closed. "There," he murmurs, and a shiver zips down my spine.

"Let me see," he orders.

I straighten, collecting myself and deciding I like the weight and feel of the necklace. It sits high, but the pieces that trail down from the main chain get longer as they reach the middle strand, which ends just above my lace-edged top.

"Creator," Breslin says with awe. "I never thought I'd see it worn again. You look a lovely thing, Sanna."

My mouth tips up at this strange alien compliment that nevertheless makes me feel radiant. "Thank you."

We're uncharacteristically quiet on the ride to town. I'm mostly in my own head until we've rolled to a stop, and Breslin hops down to tie Meesahrah to the hitching post. He also has to muzzle and hobble her because he says he can't trust her not to cause trouble in public.

I don't point out that he can't trust her to behave in private either. We all know—Meesahrah especially—that for the most part, he likes a little attitude. And she enjoys giving it. For the safety of innocent bystanders though, this is a necessary step. We could have taken one of his more placid, excellently trained animals—but Meesahrah would have had a tantrum if she'd been left behind.

She's got this big alien wrapped around her stomping hooves.

When Breslin's finished, he comes back for me. "Allow me to help you get off. Hands on my shoulders."

He means nothing dirty by this command, so I wish I could follow his order without thinking bad things. But it's impossible. I grab his wide, strong shoulders and getting off is *exactly* what I envision. I imagine getting off in all the ways. Even the wagon is included in my fantasies; it's an accessory—like sex furniture made of wood and metal instead of foam and leather.

"Good salk," he murmurs as he sets me on my feet, and the way he says it... not for the first time, I can see why he's an excellent trainer. His praise is like verbal manna. His commands are gateways to more praise. I'm helpless to resist anything his pretty voice tells me to do.

Someone calls, "Sanna! It's so good to see you!" and it takes me a second to place the person.

"Hi, Fellmoor," I say with wave in his general direction. I hear boots moving rapidly towards us on what sounds like a boardwalk but when Breslin cups me to his side, the footsteps stop abruptly.

I'm delighted—and stunned. Sometimes I've wondered why the men here treat Breslin so friendly when he's downright brusque to them. When he's training, he uses his beautiful trainer voice, and with me he has a similar, carefree way of speaking but for anyone else—anyone else *male*—he's got rotten customer service skills.

Perhaps his skills are fine and he's been warning other guys away.

He's Meesahrah keeping herdmates *(competition)* from getting too close.

I don't have much experience with a male like Breslin; none really—back on Earth, guys had a tendency to make me feel suffocated. Coddling me to death like me being blind meant that I needed to be taken by the arm and be led around (i.e. dragged, tripping and stumbling to keep up and keep my balance). It was like they couldn't fathom how someone without sight could manage the trials of each day without someone hovering.

Breslin's hovering over me right here, right now, but it's not smothering—it's possessive. Not in a controlling way. Not in a bad way. It's also decidedly *not* platonic. Breslin's touch isn't polite or remote. His arm is wrapped snugly around my back, his hand is gripping my hip, and the sound vibrating over me—*through* me—isn't coming from Kota's throat where it would be acceptable—it's Breslin that's growling.

Over *me*. And my stars in heaven is it sexy as all get out.

The way he's holding me, the way he's got himself squared in Fellmoor's direction, the *sound* he's making? This is nothing like the affectionately exasperated noise he makes at Meesahrah. This is less 'you're being a pest' and more 'I'll pop your skull like a tick's belly.' His communication is clear warning: *BACK AWAY FROM* MY *FEMALE*.

It's crazy, but this is making me feel protected—something I've never experienced before. I've had guys back home make me feel handicapped, and that's not a great feeling. Not at all. But this? I like it. Breslin's growling over me and squeezing me to his side and making me feel *female*, like *his* female, and that's a whole different thing.

"Uh, bye, Sanna," Fellmoor calls a little nervously.

"Bye," I answer with a weak and goofy little wave.

Breslin's body turns towards mine, and the vibrations rumble to a stop. Kota makes a small huffing sound and I hear her tags clack like she's looking up and judging me. *It's okay when* he *growls at people?*

Sorry, Kota: it's very, very okay when Breslin growls at people.

When Breslin's chin brushes the top of my head and rests there, heavy, hard, and hot—my brain melts. My breasts feel heavier and my back arches into his heavy arm still banded around me and the area between my legs is reacting directly to this alpha male stimuli he's throwing off. I wasn't expecting him to go territorial over me—but I am so, so into it.

Wagons roll by in the street behind us; unimportant activity and low-toned conversations passing us by. Breslin speaks into my hair. "Are you a town creature?"

My immediate, silent answer is a solid *I'll be anything you want me to be.* I manage to pull myself together enough to try for something less sex attacksical. "I live in the city. Why?"

"You seem comfortable here. I wasn't sure if you preferred the bustle or if it would disturb you. It disturbs me," he shares.

"Oh. I wouldn't say I have a preference now, but this I'm used to. The noise, the people, the hurry to get from point *a* to point *b*."

He doesn't speak, and when the pause stretches out, I add, "It's an idiom where I'm from. Like on a map, a 'from here to there' kind of thing. Hey! We could coin it here: *stick a* to *stick b*. Very catchy, *wood*'nt you say?"

"Sasspot," escapes half muttered, half feigned-exclamation, right before he gives me an affectionate squeeze.

I lose his touch from the top of my head when he starts walking. But he doesn't drag or pull on me; he just takes my hand and we walk in the same direction, hand in hand. He can't know how standout the whole experience feels for me. "Do you prefer city?"

I shrug, and Breslin's grip momentarily stiffens. "When I finally convinced my family I was capable of surviving on my own, living in the city was easiest. I can't drive a vehicle so the grocery store and the bank and my job all had to be within walking distance."

"You can drive a vehicle now," he points out. "Excellently, in fact."

My smile is bittersweet. And not because of the fact that Earth will never let me drive a wagon around my city—any city.

It's the realization that if my (spaceship) ride home shows up right now, I'll be crushed. I'm not *ready* to go home.

I'm not sure how to feel about this.

I lean hard into the solidness that is Breslin. I try to inject my earlier *laissez-faire* attitude into my voice and I manage about a quarter of it. "Well, I wouldn't be allowed to take a cart and predator alien horse around Earth's cities but it's the thought that counts."

A heavy weight drops on me again—not emotionally, but literally. Breslin's resting his cheek on top of my head. The backs of my thighs tighten and my toes curl in response.

The happy chemicals flood me when his mouth moves against my hair. "I don't like seeing your smile dim." His lips press down on my head.

I twitch hard. *Breslin kissed me* and I just had a mini orgasm or a seizure.

Oblivious to my condition, he straightens. "Let's get you fed before you starve, and then you can tell me what you did for work." He takes my hand and I let him lead me to the restaurant.

Does reciting sports stats help women calm down the hormone surges or is that just for men? I need to find out, and then I might have to learn about sports. "I have a looong way to go before I starve."

Breslin misses a step. "Do your kind's bodies store up fats and nutrients?"

I wave my hands, indicating all of myself. "Can't you see it on me?"

"Can YOU?" Breslin's tone is disbelieving. "Woman, I hate to tell you this, but I believe you're *blind*."

"Aww, you flatterer, you."

"You are *not* fat," he insists with a severity that's totally lost on me because it's warming my heart.

I go for a full-on hug. "Thank you. I've decided I'm not going to argue with you about this."

His body relaxes over mine, enveloping me. His voice is rough. "You couldn't even if you wanted to. I don't fight with females. I've learned it's a waste of my time."

I pull back a little. "Really? You're lucky Meesahrah can't talk. Pretty sure she'd tell a very different story."

A hand spans my ribs. "Behave."

I wonder if he really thinks that'll work. "Of course. I'm just pointing out the facts, Master."

Lips brush my ear, and I go still.

His voice is filled with a dangerous dash of warning—and I like it a whole lot. *"Do you know what happens to mouthy salks?"*

His hand pats my butt like he does in the morning to get my attention—just once, but it's enough to scramble my brain.

Mini Seizure—or orgasm—*number two commencing.*

"Don't make me tie you up and muzzle you next to Meesahrah."

Breathlessly I inform him, "That's not really a threat where I'm from. Tying down a woman and gagging her has kind of become popular foreplay."

Breslin disappears from my side. "Are you saying true?"

I snicker, imagining he's reared back in shock. "I am," I confirm.

"I'll be kritted." The amazement in his tone is clear. "Well don't tempt me, you insouciant little fire-lung." His hand lands on my back again, but midway this time, feeling more polite and gentlemanly. "I won't be gagging you: count yourself lucky that food puts me in a forgiving mood."

I smirk to myself. *I will do no such thing.*

CHAPTER 22

BRESLIN

Gallantly, I pull out her chair but I say under my breath, "Be good in public, *Meesahrah*."

I'm expecting her to smile at the very least. Pleasure fills me when she tips back her head and laughs from her belly. It's such a free sound. Such a musical sound.

She takes her seat, and Kota walks under the table and lays at Sanna's feet.

I'm pushing Sanna's chair in when the tavern owner himself ambles over, pleased to see me and more pleased to see the woman at my side. "I've heard all about you, miss. I'm so glad to serve you here." His voice turns teasing. "Is the Garthmaw giving you trouble?"

In the falsest, meekest voice I have ever heard, Sanna says, "Let's just say he's shown me the whip."

I blink down at her in shock. "Really? Do you think I'd take lip like this if I was wielding a whip?"

Sanna sends me the biggest, most innocent smile—and it takes first prize for the falsest one I've ever seen. Anyone can tell this female is pure trouble.

The tavern owner gives a rusty laugh and slaps his hand down on the table. In reaction to the sound or the action, Kota crawls forward, passively-aggressively laying herself protectively over our feet. She's freakishly warm. I've touched pelts yes, but I've never had a furry creature press itself on me before. It's no wonder she pants all the time, she's in constant danger of melting otherwise.

A server hustles to us, but his interest is far from harmless curiosity as he approaches, shamelessly ogling Sanna like she's the first female he's ever seen.

I know for a fact she isn't: the tavern owner's wife stops by on a semi-regular basis.

Setting a glass of water in front of her, he asks, "What's your name, miss?"

He doesn't have a drink for me. He doesn't even glance in my direction.

She places both of her hands on the edge of the table, and propels them forward slowly until the fingers of her left hand meet the glass. "Sanna."

The owner looks from his employee's far-too-interested expression to Sanna's polite one and pipes in with a light, "This is the Garthmaw's bride."

That's when the server stops moongazing at Sanna and notices me. He promptly trips back as he lowers his head a fraction.

"You misheard. I'm hosting Sanna for Ekan," I inform the tavern owner. His polite smile disappears. He takes the server by the neck and hauls him back behind the bar.

Sanna senses their retreat just as if she could physically watch them.

"Why'd they take off like that?" she whispers. "They didn't even ask what we wanted to eat."

"They'll be back." But the flirting is at an end. "They left because no one steals from a Na'rith but a Na'rith."

CHAPTER 23

SANNA

After we order, the meal almost magically appears.

"Try this, Sanna," Breslin rumbles and I feel something thin and flaky press against my bottom lip.

I've had people try to feed me, and I really wish they wouldn't. It embarrasses me a little; do they think I can't do it on my own? I'm not in the process of adapting to my blindness: I'm adept at being blind. It's all I've ever known, and I do just fine.

But Breslin's approach does not at all make me feel like he doubts my capability. The timbre of his voice and his nearness are putting me in a distinctly receptive state too, so without question I open for him.

The thing tastes like malted vinegar and has an unexpected, shreddable, stringy texture I vaguely associate with vegetable squash.

"Like it?"

I tip my head. "Yeah. I think so."

He chuckles. "You'll love dessert."

I scoff. "Of course I'll love dessert. That's the best part of every meal."

I can almost *see* Breslin shaking his head. "So you've said before. Females and their love of treats."

The *dessert-is-the-best-part* discussion is one we've had quite a few times since I came to the farmhouse. He is an alien that, thankfully, has a sweet tooth of his own and he keeps a fully stocked goodies pantry, so I haven't morphed into a ravening beast.

And trust me, if the man didn't have sweets to share, I would have.

147

"Speaking of females," I start. "A little off topic, but you've introduced me to quite a few people in my time here, and most everyone's been super nice. Your people are incredibly welcoming and just... good. But they're all *men*. All of them. Where *are* the women?"

Breslin finishes crunching down on something, and I hear his glass lift before it plunks down. It sounds empty, and I have just a second to think that before our server is apologizing and easing in to refill our drinks.

I seek out my glass, take a sip, and with my free hand I locate the spot where I need to return it, keeping my hand as a placemarker until I get my drink back in its spot.

We thank him, and Breslin says, "There are still some in the capitol. All but a few females live there. Occasionally they'll choose to dally in the outland areas but we rarely keep their attention for long... despite our body chemistry's best efforts," he adds on a wry tone. "The government used to pay women to come and stay this far out, but when they stopped, so did the supply of wives." He pauses and I hear him take another bite. "There's nothing glamorous about farming and we're too far from attractions to be of interest."

"But," I start. "It's such a rich way to experience life."

Breslin's fingers catch mine—his lightly dusted with the flavorful spices of what he was eating. "It's a *simple* life. It's not for everyone."

"What happens if women don't come out here?"

Breslin's slow to release me, almost as if he's reluctant, but he sets my hand palm down and gives it a tap before I hear him crunching again on his food. Mouth full, he manages, "Then most of our generation will die off alone."

I'm horrified.

He must see it. "Maybe the government will realize they need us after all and they'll promote the wonders of pioneering and women will show up in droves. Maybe another planet will take over this one and fill it up with their own people as settlers. Those of us who farm—"

"Or train cool animals," I cut in.

"Or train... cool... animals," he adds slowly, and I get the sense he's working over the translation, probably thinking of the literal reference to temperature, not the *impressive* definition. "We can't change women's perceptions; if they don't like farming, then they don't like farming. That's that. Men have tried to bring wives but they rarely get to keep them; the females of our kind tend to desire a more exciting lifestyle than what we can offer here."

Robotically, I take another bite of my food, using the more solid globbed thing (alien potatoes? Bland but filling, whatever it is) as a buffer to herd the little pieces I think of as avocado-corn (for their nutty flavor but little squared sizes) onto my spoon.

Patrons mill around us. Kota's chin rests on top of my feet.

Someone bumps into our table—and rushes to apologize. So polite.

Everyone's so nice here. These are hardworking, good men. Lonely men.

The thought that most women I know would kill for guys like these plays at the back of my mind. I mean, not every woman would want to live on a farm, Breslin's not wrong about that, but a tiny, crazy voice in the back of my mind whispers that if the Na'riths stole the *right* women... maybe their selling-humans plan wouldn't be *all* bad.

A tiny wash of guilt tries to rise up—but the server interrupts. "What would you like for dessert, Sanna?"

"Ooooh, dessert!" I clap happily before inclining my head towards Breslin. "Let's see if Breslin can guess what I'll like best."

Dryly, Breslin declares, "The day I try to guess a female's mind is the day I've lost my own."

I turn back to our server. "It means he doesn't know."

"Feisty salk," Breslin says under his breath. To the server, he says, "Bring one of everything, and two slices of the custard pie."

I smile in the waiter's direction. "I like his idea too much to argue—"

"That's a first," says Breslin.

"I'd kick you right now," I tell him, "If I wasn't afraid I'd catch Kota by accident." Over Breslin's chuckle, I inform the waiter, "His desserts go right here," and I pat the area on my side. "He doesn't deserve any of his own. And please and thank you for mine!"

CHAPTER 24

BRESLIN

Sanna samples everything, but when she arrives at the custard pie, I watch her devour it and it pleases me in a way I've never experienced—giving her satisfaction is intensely gratifying.

I nearly choke in my amusement when she pushes her abandoned desserts at me in some sort of silent trade—because her next action is to stalk the sound of my fork on *my* custard plate. Little thief!

Trying not to grin, I groan as if the taste hitting my mouth has put me in the throes of ecstasy.

Sanna twitches and sniffles a little.

I goad her. "Creator this is *good*."

The whimper I hear could almost be from Kota, but it's from Sanna's own lips right before her spoon dives for my pie.

I bring my fork tines down and pin her ravening utensil. "You have atrocious manners!" I chastise, but the sound of scraping followed by the chink of my plate being tipped alerts her to what I'm doing.

She uses her freed spoon to verify that I've dropped my slice onto her plate.

She's not laughing anymore. "You're sharing with me?"

"Sharing? Salk, I gave you the whole thing." *Just like my kritted heart.* I drain my glass, desperately swallowing down the words. I've heard rut makes a male chase his female of choice hard, but I won't have Sanna feeling trapped.

To occupy myself, I snatch one of her abandoned desserts, biting off the same end she tasted from, and find it almost as sweet as I imagine her lips to be.

"You didn't need to give me the whole thing, Breslin."

Too late. "Take it, Sanna." I roll my shoulders back, trying to ease the tension I feel. "I'm glad to see you happy. It'll have to tide me over for a time. We're about to spend a few days apart." Her spoon clatters to her plate, pie untouched. "My reactions to other males around you are getting sharper-edged—and it's only going to get worse. I'm going into rut."

Now she pushes her prized treat aside entirely. "So many questions," she says in a grave tone. I'm ashamed of how gratified I am when the first concern she voices is: "You're sending me away?"

I clap my hand on the table, not meaning to be loud, and not intending to add force to my words, just conviction. Still, a momentarily alarmed Kota huffs at me before she resettles herself over our feet. "I *should* have set that in motion. I should have Commed Ekan. He would have made the trip. It's too late now; I'll bunk in one of the wagons in the barn."

Sanna grimaces. "It's going to be that serious? That can't be very comfortable."

Only the embrace of her body will be accepted as comfort while I'm in rut but it feels uncivilized to put it so plainly. "I can assure you it will be no joking matter—and comfort is a limited commodity in the state I'll be in."

She takes my hand, and I enjoy her touch even as I grow a little too hungry for it. I study her with a ravenous intent, watching sorrow and compassion mingle over her features. She's imagining me suffering, and although she's right to fear that I will, I'd rather spare her the unpleasantness. I set her hand over her discarded spoon's handle. "Don't worry over me. It happens every few seasons to every male."

She doesn't pick it up. "Unless you... mate?"

"Unless I have my lifemate. A male suffers through his seasons of rut until he joins with his lifemate. Don't let the dessert go to waste, Sanna, I want you to have what makes you happy."

CHAPTER 25

SANNA

'Sanna, I want you to have what makes you happy.'

He makes me happy. And I don't want what we have between us to go to waste but I can't tell him this because he's not here.

Last night, as we digested our meal, Breslin took us to the town's music hall. I couldn't believe how skillfully the farmers assembled there played: I felt like I was sitting in the middle of an orchestra.

"They have a pretty salk to play for. It's putting them in fine form," Breslin had told me warmly.

What a sweet thing to say.

We couldn't stay long though. Leaning into Breslin and reaching up for his ear, I found it folded tightly closed. It opened under my hand, feeling like living silk petals, and I tried not to shout into it even as I tried to be heard. "The music's beautiful, but it's louder than what I'd prefer to subject Kota to. I'm sorry—can we go?"

To my suprise, Breslin had almost gone slack—I hadn't realized how tense his thigh had been against mine, or how his muscles had been strained—until they suddenly weren't anymore. "I didn't want to cut your enjoyment short, but I'm driven to attack every male here," he admitted.

Without fuss, we exited, freed Meesahrah, and trotted home.

Back at the farm, Breslin commenced with the nightly routine of checking the animals, and he told me to go on to bed. He didn't even step inside the house to retrieve his pillow and blanket. "I'll use saddle blankets. Go inside, Sanna. Sleep well."

I tried to hit the sack, but I couldn't seem to get comfortable, and I wiggled all over, until finally I nodded off into a restless form of sleep.

I startled awake, feeling myself being dragged across the bed. Too shocked to even call out for Kota, I floundered only until my body met Breslin's hard chest. And *that*. That was what I'd been missing.

Breslin's big, soft ear crushed against mine as he smooshed our faces together. The furrows on his cheek added interesting texture, but overall they didn't feel strange. They felt like Breslin. Relaxing against him, I'd whispered, "You okay?"

He'd inhaled at the top of my head, making my toes curl. "Better now," he'd growled.

When I woke up, he was gone. Besides the nightime hugging, we did not act on any feelings. Not any. He claims he's going into an oversexed alien rut and he *still* behaves? He's got the Krav Maga blackbelt of abstinence skills.

I don't. I mean, sure, I behaved last night but I was also half-waiting for him to be overcome with alien hormones and jump me. Instead, he was—yet again—the perfect gentleman.

Because he's letting me choose: him or home.

Last night, as I struggled to fall asleep in an empty, cold bed, I didn't like the trial run of No-Breslin. And I've been circling it for awhile, trying to come to terms with the fact that I want Breslin, and I want him even more than I want to go home.

I've accepted it. I'm going to stay.

I feel like I should go to Breslin with a proposal. Make it special. So I dig out that first outfit I wore that Breslin cursed Ekan for sending with me—the same one that made Breslin go momentarily speechless.

Before I slip into it—sans panties, because I've got plans—I go about starting meal prep in my night clothes. Cooking can always be a bit of a tricky adventure but this mixing bowl barely fits in my arms so it's no easy thing to get ingredients stirred. It has one sturdy handle but because it was designed by giants *for* giants it takes both of my hands to heft it up by this and as I toss in ingredients it's not like it's getting any freaking lighter.

I sniff three jars before I find the last spice I want to add. Breslin mentioned that it works great as a garnish for this meat-and-root cold-salad type dish he's taught me how to make. It feels like I'm making enough of it to satisfy the hunger of a thousand soup kitchen lines, but in reality Breslin can polish this much off by himself. If he didn't stealth-pack a lunch this morning before he slipped away he's got to be starving.

With no cell phone to call him, I leave the food and take a quick walk with Kota to determine where Breslin is at. As I suspected, he's nowhere close by that I can tell, and the place he hangs the axe is empty.

I fit the lid on the food and direct Kota to lead me to the handcart Breslin made for me. It's like a four-wheeled wheelbarrow with two shorter wheels in rear to allow me to lift it up and push it—or if whatever I'm carting around is super heavy, I can shove it along on all four wheels.

Breslin made it so that I can keep my balance and carry things at the same time.

Gosh he's nice.

I opt to push the cart and I keep Kota's handle gripped in my hand along with the cart's handle as we set out for the far pasture.

Kota grumbles anxiously about our mode of transport at first, just in case I forgot that we're walking a cart with us, but when I tell her we're looking for Breslin she focuses on it like it's her job and encourages me with yips and whines and leads me forward, guiding me around trees and keeping us walking on a nice pasture path.

When I hear the sounds of wood being chopped, I know we've made it.

But now that we're here, despite the extra slow walk thanks to lugging the food, I still don't know what to say to Breslin.

Turns out, I don't have to say much.

Hearing the axe sink into a log, I barely get the bowl moved onto the flatbed's wagon bench when arms circle me and tug me right off of my feet.

Kota gives a confused growl of protest.

"She's fine, Kota," Breslin assures her—but if *I* were Kota, I'm not sure I'd believe him.

He does not sound like himself.

His voice is rougher, his arms are like steel bands around me, and with his erection digging into my lower back? I'm in danger of grinning like an idiot. Breslin is *huge.*

I suck in a fluttery breath. "Kota, let me take off your harness and you can play."

Breslin sets me down to free Kota, and I hear something zip through the air—a stick I'll bet, she loves chewing up sticks and her happy bark tells me I'm right.

Breslin likes to toss them for her when she's not working and when his workday is done but he only gives her one throw—then I'm dragged backward into Breslin. Teeth nip my shoulder and I gasp. I don't want Kota to get upset, so I turn around and cover my mouth against his shirt and sink into his embrace as he nibbles and licks. He eagerly grinds his hips into my chest. He's tall enough he could get himself off between my boobs if I were naked and I leaned over a little.

"*What* are you doing here?" he growls into my neck.

I shiver happily in his arms. "I've decided I don't like being apart from you. We shouldn't separate anymore. It's only been part of a day but I've *missed* you."

The spikes along his jaw drag over my cheek, my ear. "I'm afraid I can't let you go now."

So far, this rut sounds terrible.

I sigh contentedly. It's my turn to nuzzle against his face. My fingers seek out his temples—

The fleshy ridged growths on either side of his head are swollen up, and he shudders as my fingers make contact.

His teeth catch one of my ears, his touch light but he inflicts a nipping sting that makes me throb. "It always breaks me a little to say goodbye. But *you,* Sanna," he nips me again, and my knees go weak, "to say goodbye to *you* would be my undoing. So tell me I don't have to say it. Tell me you'll stay."

My insides basically do the muppet dance.

Breslin rests his forehead on top of mine. *"I NEED you,* Sanna. *Please* be ready," he breathes.

"For what?" I choke out, dying for the wildness I hear in his voice.

"For me to claim you. I *need* to. I can't go slow. Not this first time."

I find his wrist cuff, and squeeze his hand. "I want you too Breslin. And I want to stay wherever you are."

Kota barks, the sound sharp and loud. Breslin disappears from me and from the sounds of it, hurls another stick and Kota thunders after it, panting happily.

Hard muscle and rough, heated skin suddenly presses against me—not pulling me into him, but backing me up, crowding me, and I'm curious and I'm about to ask what he's doing when my back connects with a tree, and Breslin's arms block me in, one on either side of my head.

As I latch onto his wrists, he growls into my throat, his nose running up and down slowly, "Be certain, salk." He nips my chin and I gasp.

Kota whines and I whimper, "Shhh,"

"Don't shush me," he growls and bites at my lips.

My knees buckle.

Breslin catches me up, one hand imprisoning my wrists and one arm snaking behind my back to yank me forward and bring me flush against him. It feels so good. It feels like *Finally!*

"San San," he groans into my hair and the heat of his body is perfect and I want to press my hips to his. I follow through with the desire, letting his grip on my wrists take my weight as I latch him with my legs and half climb him.

With an alien snarl, Breslin drags my arms around his neck, lifts my butt, and tosses up my skirt.

He grabs my knee, brings my thigh higher over his hip and I squeal when I feel hardness the temperature of a steel forge bumping against my entrance. I feel a spurt against me, and I'm confused: did he just come on me?

"What?" Breslin asks, panting.

I bite my lip, suddenly having so many questions pop up. "When did you get your pants down?"

His breath steams over my cheek. "Really?"

The tension and amusement straining his voice makes my scalp tingle and my insides clamp down on nothing. The empty flutter makes me moan, and the desperate sound seems to break Breslin. I feel him go tense everywhere under my touch.

I don't know what I thought would happen when I went in search of an alien who *warned* me he was in the grip of rut, but I don't expect him to ram himself into me like a wild creature. There's another burst of jelly-like liquid from him that helps him gain entry, but he's so much bigger than I'm used to. His immense thickness fills my belly with what feels like a white-hot branding rod and he groans as I shriek.

Kota barks.

"NOT. NOW," Breslin grits out in the sternest voice I've ever heard him use.

With a sad whine, Kota goes quiet.

His ferocity is shocking, but I've had foreplay for what feels like weeks. My system responds as each and every dirty fantasy I've entertained since I met him becomes my wild reality. My insides sing—and get wetter. I wriggle as slickness gathers, the hardness stuffed inside me softening my muscles, my innermost flesh melting in response to his hunger.

I feel a hot jet hit my insides like a happy punch. Again, I pause.

Breslin doesn't.

It's like he's busting even as he surges into me with primal hunger, our skin slapping obscenely loud. I can feel myself dripping around his base. Pinned on him like I am, my head comes to about the middle of his chest. I'm surrounded by him, enveloped by his broad body and impaled on his hardness. Bark digs into my back, and I'm limited with how much I can move against him in this position so I end up taking his battering more than riding him until his hands close around my feet.

He grabs my heels and warns me, "Hold on."

He starts rocking into me—not bouncing me up and down, but working into me in a back and forth motion that's stimulating the front wall of my vagina in a way I've never experienced before.

Then again, I've never been railed by an alien against a tree before, so that might be why this feels completely new and so brain-meltingly dirty.

Bracing more of my weight in his palms, and letting my butt beat a rhythm on the tree behind me, I feel a thrill as an orgasm with the strength of a tsunami gathers inside me, heat and light and desperate hunger filling my pelvis and making me whimper as I work myself in time with his rocking.

When it breaks my mind goes white.

I can actually see the color. I've always heard it described as an absence, but this is a blinding shock of spotlight, highlighting everything in my entire world: the mammoth proportions of Breslin cradling me, inhaling his musk as he works himself in a way that's teasing out my pleasure, his heart slamming fast and powerful as it beats under my ear.

Leaning back, he crowds over me. My skin flutters as—is he *licking* my shoulder?

He nudges my head to the side using his cheek and those spikes at his jaw poke and scrape against my skin. My thigh muscles tighten and another shock of ripples happen in my stomach as more spurts bathe my insides.

But he's still hard. Stunned, I don't react when he carries me away from our tree. When he sets me down I feel the slats of the wagon seat under my butt, hear the creak of it as he tugs and slides me where he wants me—which does all sorts of interesting things with him still inside me.

"Lie back," he orders.

When his tongue laps at my throat, I tilt my head back, giving him more access. Letting him taste me. I'm still overwhelmed that this is really happening.

I'm loving every second of it.

And with every pass of his rough textured tongue against my skin, I squirm.

His hips flick in response, and the wagon creaks.

He does it again.

And again. I'm panting. The smell of varnished wood under me, the salty chips-and-Island fruit rinds sweat-tanged man over me, the creak of the wagon joints as Breslin's thrusts rock us: I revel as he bangs me.

My head bumps something—the bowl of food, I realize—and I want to bring a hand up to slide it away but I can't because I'm caught, muscles so tense they're shuddering, the pressure inside me building, *building.*

Bresin spurts inside me again and I come so hard I nearly scream.

He pulls out, still hard.

Panting, shuddering, I can't close my legs because I don't have the strength. His big hands haven't left me so I don't feel an overwhelming need yet—and when Breslin drags my hips closer, I realize he's not done.

My butt is cushioned only by a little fabric, my skirt rumpled beyond saving, I'm sure, as he drags me to the edge of the wagon.

"Perfect," he breathes—and I'd ask him "Perfect for what?" but he's breathing on my pussy and my mouth falls open in a silent cry as his tongue drags over my swollen flesh. His strange ears have flattened, smoothing along my skin like crushed flower petals. When the ridges on the side of his head bump my inner thigh he full-body twitches.

Groaning, Breslin digs his head harder into my leg, his temple dijjü feeling puffed and hot. He's rocking a little against me, and operating on instinct, I close my thighs around his head.

It turns him savage.

Apparently, dijjü are a bit like clits. Weird but cool. A little gentle friction against the insides of my legs and he's bucking his mouth on me and pinning my lower half in place with one of his big arms thrown over my stomach.

He eats me out with abandon. His enthusiasm might end me but I'll die happy and I know it. My thighs shaking, I come again and again, and by the time he tones down to slow sucks and gentle licks I'm incoherently whimpering, begging, twitching, shuddering.

Breathless, dazed, I can't do anything but lie back as he grasps me by the hips and feeds his cock into me again. His thrusts nudge me along until he has to chase me, closing his hands over my shoulders to keep me in place until he ruts another wet climax, his seed pooling under me when he unplugs us and pulls out.

As I struggle to remain conscious, he rips open my blouse so he can take hold of my breasts, kneading them, tweaking my nipples, tasting them. Then he clambers up, positions me on the bench where he wants me, and finishes fucking me like he's taking ownership of everything I have left.

When he comes this time, it's with a long, loud roar that has me quaking—especially on the inside as heat fills me and *floods* out as he softens.

Kota leaps up on the wagon and with a disgusted sounding huff, I hear her settle herself on the floor area like she feels we've just defiled the bench.

We did. And it was *awesome*. I grin like a loon.

Breslin pets along my stomach, teasing my skin and making it flutter and jump under his divinely rough fingers. He seems very content. This was a *claiming*. "Do you live?"

I can't move. "Barely."

His chuckle is wicked.

"How are you feeling?" I pant.

"Infinitely improved," he says, sounding delightfully vainglorious.

I smile. I might never be able to walk again but this. Was. *Worth*. It.

I pet his strange bumps for hair and he hums. I play with his dijjü and he stiffens inside me again.

He grunts and hugs me tight.

I fit my fingers to his cheek grooves and guide him for a kiss, tasting myself on him.

With the fingers of my other hand, I continue to tease and trace his inflamed temples, and I feel his jaw tighten, the muscles under my hand jumping.

"Mmm," I purr. "Someone feels ready for round two."

Meesahrah honks and the wagon rolls forward a hair, just enough for me to squeak and Breslin to groan.

I imagine her gaping at us this whole time, head turned with one eye trained on all the action. Now that her shock has worn off I guess she deems our interlude over.

Breslin pulls out of me, and my eyes cross. I'm so swollen, I feel *everything*.

"Do I smell food?" he asks, pressing a kiss to my forehead.

I wave in the bowl's general direction. "Mmmhmm."

He nudges my thigh with his ever ready-to-go-again *and again* penis. "Rouse yourself and eat. You'll need your strength if I'm going to take you from now and all night."

CHAPTER 26

SANNA

By the time Breslin's rut ends, my lazy concern was not unfounded: I can barely walk. But I can sure ride—and when he lets me emerge from the bed, I feel qualified to tackle a ride of a whole different sort—because while the prospect of taking a tumble off an alien may not be an appealing one, I now have confidence that I can hold my own when it comes to sitting astride one.

Meesahrah, for all that she's a brat, really seems to like me. And despite her tendency to suck my clothing, fingers, hands, and my arms into her mouth, I like her too. She also chases the other Narwari away from me when I walk through the pasture. When Breslin witnessed it, he was stunned. He told me it's what Narwari females do when they've got a new foal.

After that, he didn't protest when I started taking Meesahrah for walks in the round pen. It's normally the place Breslin gives the Narwari a light warm up before he harnesses them. I've been using it to work myself up before I climb on.

Breslin's been adding a thicker layer of substrate to the round pen—'padding,' he calls it—just about every day. If I hurtle down, it really will be an easy landing. But the stuff is so soft and so fine that every one of my footsteps sinks into it, so each day's been more and more of a workout for me just to walk.

I'm two circles in with Meesahrah on one side and Kota on my other, me slogging between them, when I hear the tell-tale creak of wagon wheels. I holler, "No more sand!" I'm choking on laughter. "You're being crazy!"

"I want it to be a gentle drop," Breslin insists.

"I thought the objective was to try *not* to fall."

"Everybody falls," he says matter of factly.

I pick up my knees higher, trying to prance through it. I puff, "Gotta pay if you want to play?"

There's a pause as he works over the idiom, then I hear the wry humor in his voice. "Said true."

"Where are you getting all this sand?"

"I dig it up here and there," he says easily.

Meesahrah noses my shoulder. She doesn't seem to be breathing hard at all, which is unreal. Speaking of unreal—so is Breslin. "You've been digging wagonloads of dirt up *yourself?*"

He sounds nonplussed. "Of course. Did you think I had piles of sand waiting for me?"

I scritch Kota between the ears, absurdly pleased that she's panting a little. Not as much as me, but at least I'm not the only one working here. "Well... yeah, we do at home."

"Where do the piles come from?"

I laugh. "I suppose somebody digs them up!"

Breslin makes a grunt that, without words, manages to say *Well see? There you go.*

I've got so much sand in my shoes, they're weighted down. At least the stuff isn't coarse like the sand from Earth. This stuff is a silty powdered sugar. Every step is the gentlest *poof* right before I sink. "I feel bad that Meesahrah is going to have my bodyweight added to her walk. It feels like we're dragging through this stuff."

Metal tines make a ringing sound as Breslin hauls out his rake to smooth his latest sand-load addition. "She drags through nothing. Her toes are split. They spread wide so she stays on top. Unlike you and I, she's made to cross sand effortlessly."

"Ahhh, *that's* why she's not breathing as hard as me. You cheat," I tell her.

She warbles at me.

"Feel ready?" Breslin asks.

I feel like even Meesahrah's waiting for my answer. She's tacked up (which was a fun process: I panicked when I learned there was no pommel/horn. Breslin however retained his level-headed reasonableness: *"But what is the purpose? If it's only attached to the saddle if—when—it slides, then so does your anchor point. That doesn't seem a sound safety measure—mind you, I'm not discounting—I'm simply struggling to picture it."* My head tilted in consternation, I'd replied, *"Great, now that makes two of us."*) and her nose rests on my shoulder, not even trying to eat my shirt in this moment. "I'm so—" *not* "—ready."

Breslin hums. "Smells like untruth."

Whoa, whoa. "You can smell lies?"

Breslin laughs. "No, but if my sense of smell was so acute what would I detect?"

I lift my chin. "That I'm *determined.*"

The rake makes a dull thunk as he must return it to the wagon. "Hence the abundance of soft sand. Prepare to ride."

I'm so nervous, even Breslin touching me isn't a sufficient enough distraction. He boosts me up, and when I swing my leg over Meesahrah's back—one of his hands bracing my shoulder, and one of them steadying my hip—I swallow bile and work to steady my balance. "Why did I want to do this?" I whimper.

"Shhh, easy. Do you want to stop?"

At his *shhh,* calm blossoms through me, and although I'm mildly terrified of the height I'm hovering at above the (soft and sandy) hard, cold ground, I *do* want to do this. "Thank you, but no—please keep talking to me though."

"Whatever you need, Sanna. I'm right here." Breslin's got this easy way of speaking, it's almost trance-inducing, and I've heard him use this on the Narwari when he's working with them.

It's totally working on me too. "Just keep hypnotizing me with your voice, and we're good," I tell him. "Tell me I won't die until I believe it."

His hand squeezes my thigh and his voice is firm and his words are final. "You will *not* die."

I manage to trust him on this and I relax. "Whew. Thanks."

He gives my thigh another squeeze, and with my nerves mostly settled, *now* his touch on me is starting to register and I really need it not to. I can't afford to be distracted by my hormones.

Meesahrah effectively steals my attention by shifting under me.

"Ah!" I yelp—quietly, because I don't want to terrify her and have her rear up and drop me and crush me under her—"

"Sanna."

I take a shaky breath.

"You're doing so well. Look at you: you're up on Meesahrah! We can stop now if you want, and this can be the end of it, or we can do this in little steps every day if you want to build up to more. But you've accomplished what you set out to do. Taste your success."

I smile in his direction. "You know that stuff all over the ground? It gets everywhere and I mean *everywhere.* So I don't want to alarm you, but it means that 'success' tastes like *sand.*"

Breslin booms with laughter, and thank goodness Meesahrah's used to it, because she doesn't so much as flinch.

Warmth fills me. There's this candy on Earth that pops as it dissolves in your mouth, and it feels like those little candies are being happy-licked along my back right now, exploding over my skin.

Kota makes a whining huff from the ground, feeling anxious and probably a little left out.

"It's alright, sal—girl," I tell her.

"Give in." Breslin pretends to demand. "Salk sounds better than that coarse *gurrl*."

My lip tips up. "You're seriously going to judge my Earthen words?"

He pats my leg before he slides his hold to my hip, anchoring his hand. "I don't have to. You already prefer the superior alternative. You just want to fight the bit."

"Gotta stop," I warn him weakly, *no* willpower around him. "Bickering is foreplay."

"Only with you. Otherwise I'd have married Meesahrah."

The area between my legs is very, very awake and this is really not the time, and really, really not the place. The spot on my body he's holding is all I can think about. "Maybe you should have. You two are perfect for each other."

"You kritted lie. We'd be miserable and she'd kill me in my sleep."

"You think she'd wait til you're sleeping?"

"At least you'd have the courtesy to warn me to my face first." He strokes his hand along the side of my butt lightly and even the backs of my ears tingle in reaction.

Someone could grab my arm and push me ahead of them going down a flight of steep, curving stairs (one of my worst fears, seriously) and I wouldn't be scared right now. Of course, if Breslin had ahold of my hip like this no one would dare push me anywhere. Or drag me. Really, Breslin's like a magic cure for my worries. I wish I'd had him years ago. I'd never know what tumbling down the steps felt like, never have a well-meaning stranger say, "Oh, sorry, I was trying to help you so you *wouldn't* fall!"

Meesahrah moves sharply and I grasp for her neck and end up with Breslin's hand. I cling to him like a buoy and clamp my legs tighter around Meesahrah. She continues to jerk under me, and I have a moment to wonder if she's seizing in laughter until the repetition of her motion helps me assemble, without tactile cues, what her movements are—she's biting at herself. She has an itchy spot. I've stood at her shoulder and felt her do this when she needs to scratch or when she gets a bug on her side.

Breslin could help her out but he's in the middle of making sure I don't lose my balance and she'll have it in a moment. For her, this is no big deal. This is normal.

Relax.

She's otherwise standing completely still—a feat almost unheard of for her—and I'm okay. I'm doing all right. And I want to try for more. "Can we try walking a little?"

Breslin's arm relaxes and his hand falls away when I stop clutching him. "Cluck when you're ready."

Inside, I'm laughing, thinking how odd the order sounds, but I know what he means. I cluck like we do when Meesahrah is supposed to walk the wagon forward.

I correct my balance when my hips suddenly feel like they're being tugged ahead of me—and it feels *so* different, the tempo of her footfalls feels so very different from up here than when I'm sitting behind her on a (virtually) unmoving wagon seat.

She has an easy, smooth gait and when I've walked next to her on the ground, or driven the wagon, I've gotten a full sense of her measured steps. But to be up here on top of her back, *feeling* her muscles flex and dip and shift: it's crazy different. My body bobs with her and even though she's only walking in a steady line, every one of her steps is equal to like five of mine and I feel like I'm *flying*.

Giddiness overwhelms me for a second and I try to rid the tension in my hands by patting Meesahrah's neck. I don't have the reins; Breslin does, and he controls Meesahrah as he walks beside us. Kota pants and from the unobstructed direction of the sound, I can tell she's looking up at me, also keeping pace with us.

"How do you like it?" Breslin asks, quietly enough not to startle me. He's amazing at this.

I've caught the timing of Meesahrah's gait and my hips automatically rock in time with her motion. It's so cool, I can't even speak.

"San San? You all right?"

I clear my throat. "It's incredible."

His hand squeezes my ankle and it feels incredible too.

I straighten a little, fear no longer locking up my shoulders, neck, spine—all of me. "I've heard people try to describe horseback riding before. They use words like 'freeing'—and I never really got it before. I never got how it could be all that different from riding in a car or walking yourself. But... it is. And it's so much better."

"I'm glad you like it."

We walk like this for several minutes and I feel my confidence building with every step.

"Ready to stop?" he asks.

"What?" My hand moves from where I have it resting on Meesahrah's shoulders and I reach out and wait for his fingers to lace with mine. "No, why?"

"Just checking. You'll have to tell me when you get tired."

"Shouldn't we ask Meesahrah?"

His thumb taps my skin. "Pah. She pulls wagons that could hold thousands of you in weight, and she can do that all day. You think walking with you is going to tire her out anytime soon? Boredom will get her first, and she's not bored. She's being very... I half believe that you snatched her personality and switched it out on me. Don't try to deny: I'll have too much a struggle to believe you."

Shoulders shaking as I try to contain my snickering—I have a slightly irrational fear that I'll scare Meesahrah up here and she'll dump me and I could die—I do deny this ridiculousness. "Oh please. Just who would I have used to switch her personality? All your animals get sassy with you."

He flicks my leg. "Maybe you switched out hers with your own. When we first met, you were so sweet. *Now* look at you."

I snigger.

We keep going, and I'm rather amazed at Meesahrah's patience too: she's probably walked around this ring a billion times—and she's already walked this ring loads of times with me before today. It must be very boring, but she's not so much as bouncing in place. And I'm ready for more. "I want to try the reins now."

"You have them," he says, laying them over my hands.

I hear a metallic snap and I know he's attaching lines to Meesahrah's bridle so that he can help control her motion and speed from the ground as I learn up top. We discussed this process at length, deciding the best way to approach this. We weren't sure how it would go.

It's going *awesome*.

The commands for riding are different than driving, and there's a lot of leg control that I didn't have the capacity to imagine. Breslin's teaching me to use my legs to communicate with Meesahrah even more than my hands feed commands through the reins.

I have a blast, and my heart feels like it's going to burst with happiness when we stop for the day and Breslin calmly talks me through tightening my far knee to help my leg make it over Meesahrah's back as he steadies me before helping me the rest of the way down.

"I did it," I crow through silly tears.

"You did. And you did well," he confirms, and his words are like hugs on my heart.

I throw my arms around his neck.

When he clutches me and turns our embrace into a slightly x-rated hug, I happily funnel my exhilaration into this impromptu sex attack. With no trees available, Breslin asks, "Can you hold yourself up by holding onto my neck?"

"Oooh, you're going to hold me up and we do this all freestyle?" I reply breathlessly, and fold my arms behind his nape, locking my hands over my elbows.

He takes up my feet in his hands, which brings my knees up from his hips to his ribs.

"Huh," he says. "Small problem."

"Yeah. We're, ah, not going to line up," I murmur. I warn him, "Don't let me fall," before I let go of my elbows and clasp my hands at his nape instead.

"Therrrre," he growls. "We can make this work."

Yes we can.

Taking advantage of our preoccupation, Meesahrah sucks up half of the back of my shirt in her mouth, and Kota loudly shares her feelings on this whole business.

When Breslin and I finish, me hugged tightly to him, I assure Kota she's fine and Breslin fists the fabric at my back to free it from his beast's teeth. That done, I smooth my skirt, and hunker down to Kota's level to love on her and fit her harness on. It's a confirmation that we're partnering up again and it's time for her to go back to work. For a guide dog, it's hard for them to want to shut off. They love their jobs. Kota's being a real champ about watching me work with Meesahrah.

She's a champ about sharing me with Breslin too. For a long time it's been just me and her, but she's adjusted and sees him as part of our family now.

"Do you hunger yet, human?" Breslin asks, and I hear the rough strike of his hand patting Meesahrah's side—it's a hollow *pong-pong* beat over her ribs and an affectionate move she adores even if it sounds alarming.

I bounce up. "Starving!"

Kota barks and I hook a thumb at her. "She says she is too."

This becomes our pattern every day after chores if Breslin doesn't have appointments. Meesahrah loves the extra attention, and we learn that she's a natural at this. I'd heard that there are all kinds of horses; ones who will listen to your cues to the letter, ones who will walk right into a wall for you if you ask them to. Because they trust you. They want to please you and obey.

And then there are horses that take your cues under advisement. If you guided them into a wall, they'd turn or stop.

Obviously, for someone like me, an animal that is sensitive to my commands yet makes executive decisions when the need arises is perfection. Meesahrah may not be a horse, but she's exactly what I need.

Breslin had me test this, very carefully letting me get too close to the sides of the ring, waiting to see how Meesahrah would react. She turns herself, not bumping into things, ultimately deciding if my command is safe to follow.

Breslin says it: "This works out grand, Sanna."

It sure does. But unfortunately, nothing can be one hundred percent easy, one hundred percent safe all the time—and so it happens. Eventually, I fall.

Sand kicks up at me as Breslin races to my side. I'm lifted to my feet so fast I lose my breath. *"Are you hurt?"*

"No," I answer shakily.

His hands are gripping onto me so tightly, and I realize he's scared. "Then why do I see tears?"

A watery chuckle trickles out of me. "Because falling is scary."

A great big sigh gusts over me right before Breslin hugs me to his chest. He's so much stronger than me, I squish against him and stick there as he grates out, "It's too late to be scared of falling. It's done. Break yourself to it." He presses his lips hard into the side of my face. "I'm glad you're not injured."

I burrow into his chest, taking refuge until my heart stops racing. It wasn't even a very big drop, not really, but man is it a scary sensation. Although, with Breslin, it doesn't feel as terrifying as I expected it to.

"I'm right with you," I say into his shirt, sounding very muffled, "I'm glad I didn't die."

Breslin squeezes me tighter. "I don't know how my parents managed to watch that happen to me more than once—Sanna, I think my kritted heart stopped."

I pat his chest. "I'm okay and don't be sorry. Everybody falls, right?"

He's draws away slowly. He's quiet so long I don't expect him to answer so I'm rocked at how softly he answers, "Yes. It seems we do."

His rough hands cup my cheeks, slide to my neck, and hold me still for an inflaming kiss.

After releasing my mouth, he grits out, "Creator, you taste good."

"Yeah? What do I taste like? Meesahrah licked my face a bit ago so I probably taste like—" I start to tease but he cuts me off, one hundred percent serious, sexily caveman.

"Mine."

CHAPTER 27

BRESLIN

Wood creaks with every grind and bump and thrust. My feet are braced on the footboard of the bed, my hands are gripping the headboard tightly enough to make my knuckles go bloodless, and I arch my back harder as I tug and and pull my body, keeping my penile stylet only half buried in Sanna's heat, my pubic bone grinding over her sensitive nodule to achieve the stimulation she likes best. Her legs are folded over my hips, her heels spur my flanks, and my nudging sets her to dancing under me again.

I jolt into her unexpectedly hard—slamming all the way in when the footboard gives out and the headboard snaps under my hands.

The shock of it makes her tighten impossibly around me, and I lose myself to the sensation with a heaving, heavy grunt.

"Did we," she gasps. "Did we just break the bed?"

"Yes," I grit out. And though I can barely think let alone speak, I need to vocalize so that Sanna is aware of what I need. "And we're not stopping."

She grabs my hips and her toes dig into the backs of my thighs, making me want to stay buried deep, keep our bodies connected, keep our souls this close to one another forever.

She clenches her inner muscles around me and I know forever is not an option. I order myself not to spill inside her yet and I manage to hold off, but Sanna feels too good for me to last long.

I give in to the urge to thrust. Grunting, growling, knowing how excited it makes her to *hear* me receiving pleasure from her body, I rock into her until I bathe her insides with another quaking rush of my seed.

Watching her come undone at my sounds, at the feel of me rutting over her, inside her—it's magnificent. She is magnificent. Pinning my hips hard to hers, I release again, liquid fire jetting out of my ducts. The mucus my stylet constantly emits for Sanna keeps her body as hungry for mine as mine is for her. *This* is the reaction Iechydmaw women used to have to Iechydmaw males. It's anyone's guess why the response is all but gone in the females of our kind—but it's full strength in my Sanna. Aroused beyond reason, I lovenip her collarbone.

She whimpers.

I roar in triumph.

Before the kick of euphoria even has a chance to dim let alone fade, I flip us, rolling to my back and popping her up above me. "Ride me, salk." I stroke her flank. "I won't buck. Much." I punctuate my statement by planting my heels and thrusting up into her, making her gasp and keel forward, almost collapsing on my chest.

Of course Ekan would choose this moment to make his grand entrance. Or *try*.

The door shudders, making both of us tense and Sanna half-jumps—which makes me fall back with a groan.

Kota makes an otherworldly noise and throws herself against the age-scarred wood, warning the intruder not to dare try their luck coming in.

Over the din comes Ekan's muffled voice after he tries and fails to shoulder it open. "What the tevek? Is this barred?" He begins to beat his fist against it.

"Give us a quarter of a stick, machaii!" I shout.

"Making us wait is no way to treat guests," he hollers back—but there's no censure. He's just being a Narwari's hind.

I snarl (and I'm amused to note, this makes Sanna shudder—and not in fear). "Guests Comm ahead. Polite for polite: now take a kritted walk!"

Ekan laughs heartily.

Sanna's been trying to rise off of me but my hands on her hips have kept her clamped in place. As all hope for the chance to have her ride me vanishes, I despair more than a little—but only one of us has to suffer. I fish between Sanna and I while she writhes and whispers a wild, *"What* are you *doing?"*

"Let's finish you off," I say, not bothering at all to whisper. "Ekan can wait."

Sanna tries to rear up but only succeeds in impaling herself on me further and making me grunt. *Maybe I'll be coming after all.*

I circle her nodule and she drops her face to gasp and shudder into my chest. When her insides squeeze me until my eyes cross, I give in to the impulse and bang into her from below until I'm seeding her once more.

Ekan raps his knuckles on the door. "An awful lot of heavy breathing going on." The teveker sounds so pleased with himself. "What are you two doing? Mate-fevered cavorting?"

"Oh for Creator's patience," I say into Sanna's hair before I lift my head to bellow, "YES! Let us get dressed, you thickskull."

"Good for you!" Ekan calls back with genuine happiness. "See you both soon then!"

"That cheery little swill-stirrer," I grouse. Gently, I lift Sanna, disengaging us with a wet squelch that has my mouth watering and my body humming for the chance to blow inside of her again. "His timing is *rotten.* But let's meet with him. There's no telling what trouble he can devise if left to his own devices."

I watch Sanna while we dress. I mean to search her features to determine if she regrets her decision to stay rather than go with Ekan—but when I see no distress, I get sidetracked. Her lips are darker from our kisses. Her hair is mussed in every direction—disarrayed from when I fisted her tresses earlier and pounded into her from behind.

I get as far as watching her breasts swing as she fights to shimmy into a tight top—and I'm hard as stone. "Krit."

"What's wrong?" she asks, wriggling her hips to settle a skirt on her lower half.

Now I could break *through* stone. "Watching you has set me to full mast. Again."

She stops. Then she ducks her head, cheeks flushing, as she snickers. "What an uncomfortable predicament."

She sashays towards me—but she must get a sense for the severity of my baser thoughts because she stops well out of my reach. "You'll have to tell it to calm down. We need to go out there and say hi."

"Come here and say hi," I tell her, voice husky.

She shakes her head. "I want to—"

"Then *come here*. I'll care for all of your wants and I vow I'll make you feel good. *Tevek*." I drag the heel of my hand down and squeeze myself until I can think. "No, no, you're right—you'd best run. Leave quickly before I pounce on you. Maybe if you're not standing here looking ready to be mounted I'll be able to wrestle this under control. Krit, one would think you own this member of mine despite me being the one to wear it."

Cheeks patched bright like some sort of alien-scarlet come-hither signals, Sanna flees from me, giggling.

When my organ calms down enough that walking will no longer be uncomfortable, I make my own exit, and I when I step outside my ears are caressed by Sanna's talented voice teasing notes out in a smooth legato. She's been singing all over the farm lately, her tree-visitor never far. This time is no exception: I watch as the yushabee drops onto her shoulder—and a shocked Ekan explodes. "THAT is a fortune in the making!"

Oh no. *No* way in kritted hell. Storming over, I cut him a warning glare.

Which he promptly ignores. "Sanna, that's quite a talent you have."

"Not my female, Ekan."

"Sanna," he says patiently. "Have you given a thought to what you'll do to keep yourself occupied here? The seasons can be long. Would you like to make a small fortune in your downtime?"

Sanna shifts—instead of *looking* between us, she listens. And she's a wise woman: she senses when a trap is being sprung and she doesn't say anything.

I do. "You may be my friend, but touch Sanna and you will be a dead one."

Ekan feigns hurt but it's a mockery—his eyes gleam as he watches the yushabee's hands and hand-like feet close over low branches to return to the tree we're assembled under. "I'm sure Sanna can make up her own mind if she wants—"

"No."

"—for the good of everyone—"

"No."

"—to gain riches beyond her wildest—"

"Ekan!" I bellow.

Sanna pats my side, and instead of snapping my friend in half, I settle for steaming him with my angry breaths.

Unfazed, Ekan grins at me, tweaks Sanna's cheek over my growl of warning, and bounces back out of my reach before snapping his fingers. "Let me show you what I came for."

"About that," Sanna starts. "I won't be going home."

Ekan waves the notion away. "You're well mated: that message was received clear when Bres held you captive and rutted you while I stood outside the door—"

I hiss at him when Sanna covers her face with her hands.

He isn't worried for his life like he really ought to be. "We'll still be going to Earth if you want us to bring you something specific, but otherwise that female-collecting venture? You could say it's taken a different turn." He grins. "Wait til you see what I've brought for this place. Tevek I give the best gifts."

"Puppies?" Sanna asks with a sweet smile.

"What are puppies?" Ekan asks, throwing open one of the Na'rith ship's bay doors.

Standing just inside are females. So many females. Females of every kind.

One of them—a *human* female—approaches us, her smile all teeth. "Lucky you. Your BF here brought you a shipfull of whores."

I gape around us. "You stole WHAT?"

Sanna gapes in the direction of the female's voice. "What did you just say?"

"Aw, did I ruin the surprise?" the woman asks, not looking sorry in the least.

Ekan herds the angry-looking female back into the ship, and the collective gives her a wide berth as he does it. "Tut tut Gracie, that's 'former brothel slaves.' Please go back where you belong and don't stir up the others for once?"

When he returns to our side, he sends me a harried look. "That female is exhausting. Be glad she declared she doesn't want to live on a planet full of farmers. Anyway, besides her, you'll love my gift—it's fantastic. I brought you *wives*."

Sanna's arms drop from me. "WHAT!"

I drag Sanna closer. "Ignore whatever he just said. He's claimed that simulated sunlight is just as good as the real thing but clearly the lack has left him with some damage."

"Sanna, Sanna," Ekan chides, "These wives aren't *for* Breslin. He's just going to help me parcel them out to farmers that will pay. Don't worry: I'll even give Bres ten percent of the cut." He looks skyward. "Females. So territorial."

The human named Gracie raises her voice enough to be heard. "Hey, I volunteer to kick his ass for you."

"No worries," Sanna promises. "I'll be happy to do it myself."

Ekan holds up his hands and looks between the humans. "What is it with this species? Such aggression."

"Why did you bring a shipfull of former slaves here?" I manage in a controlled and level tone.

"We promised to do our best to get them happily paired off as beloved wives to lonely, doting farmers who will treat them like treasured princesses for the rest of their days."

"That does sound nice," Sanna concedes. "IF that's what they want."

"It's perfect. And this," Ekan throws his arms out and turns in a circle, "This is the perfect place! No one will *ever* look here."

He stops and scratches his chest as he takes in his surroundings, grimacing ever so slightly in a way that suggests that there's nothing at all before him as far as the eye can spy save for farmland, leafy pissing posts and livestock. He ignores the females that are peering out of the ship's belly in curiosity, and he sets off for the house.

The krit of it is: he's right—about the fact no one will show up here to search for stolen slaves anyway. This planet's farmers don't have access to ships to shuttle off and buy up women. No one will suspect this place of harboring stolen females. "Where did you get them all?"

Without asking for an invitation, Ekan shoulders open the door and steps inside, heading for the icebox. He's always hungry, and he pulls out a platter of cold cuts that Sanna prepared for *me*. "We acquired them from pleasure houses here and there." Stuffing his mouth full to free up his hand, he plants his fist in the center of my chest, a gesture peculiar to Na'rith's as far as I've found, and meets my gaze with one of the most serious expressions I've ever witnessed Ekan be capable of. "If you could visit some of your neighbors and start discreetly asking around," he swallows his bite of food, "we'd like to get these lovelies paired off. We've promised them we'll try another planet if they don't find what they're looking for here—but believe me, the sooner we can unload, the better for ship-domicile relations."

"Trouble in paradise?" Sanna asks, her tone flavoring the air with irony.

Ekan groans dramatically. "You humans may not have much in the way of a developed sense of smell, but you sure can detect the scent of a stray female." He gestures widely in my direction. "Take note, Bres. Don't let yourself get cornered by one of Sanna's rivals. Pro tip? *Any* stray female is your female's rival. Heed my words, friend."

He reaches for another bite, but stops with the hunk of meat suspended over his mouth when he catches sight of our bed—the head and footboards looking like they were blown off. "Upstagers!" Ekan exclaims. "After Beth spawns, we should chain her to our beds until we break them!"

EPILOGUE

BRESLIN

Iechydmaw men fall all over themselves to prove to the females that they will make good mates. For two days, unbeknownst to me, Ekan charges the men to rent out my flashiest Narwari and my nicest wagons for countryside rides so the ladies can get a feel for the place.

Up until I saw him counting credit sticks I thought I was being hospitable for free.

"Have you no shame?" his woman, Beth, asks him.

"This isn't for me," he protests. "Think of it as a congratulatory nuptials gift for a bed well broken."

"Bed well broken...?" Beth stares at the most deranged of her mates in confusion before turning her gaze on Sanna.

As if she can sense it, Sanna's cheeks flush.

Beth's eyes fly to me. *"Wowww..."*

Ekan shoves the creditsticks at me and takes Beth by the shoulders. "We have to break their record."

Beth gestures to us. "How do you top that? We can make it *good,* but they kinda did it first—"

Her eyes go wide as Ekan swoops in and he attacks her mouth. He only lets the poor pregnant woman up so he can proclaim, "They broke a bed; *we'll collapse one!*"

Over sticks and sticks (or weeks and weeks, as Sanna calls the passage of time) Sanna does an excellent job as matchmaker, using her knowledge of the friends she's made here to suggest males whose personalities would complement the women she gets to know.

185

The women are smitten with our Iechydmaw style of gentle courting. They're *delighted* when their besotted admirers' dijjü start swelling for them.

Having a sudden abundance of women to take out and spoil has made our little town grow—and one of the females opens up a dress shop. It's an instant success and more business ventures are predicted to follow as these women discover or rekindle personal talents and hobbies.

Having their ship empty of all the drama that evidently came with housing a mass of females, the Na'riths are in high spirits and I press my advantage with a grateful Ekan, asking for a favor. I'm aware that the Gryfala are keeping a settlement of humans and to provide for them, they hired the Na'riths to obtain necessary supplies from Earth. I hoped to purchase provisions too. Some out of the ordinary.

Ekan delights in odd quests and his eye for rare things means he's taken quite an interest in this venture. This day marks their return, and although Sanna's aware of their impending arrival, she has no idea what gifts the Na'riths will be bearing.

She's singing to her yushabee when their ship lands in the pasture, scattering decoy Narwari while the rest of the pack rapidly configures themselves in a classic staggered formation known as a *hunting net*. Meesahrah immediately goes to work trying to pry at the aft fuel cell access panel. I bellow for her to leave off. The Na'riths will be understandably unamused if she manages to cause any damage.

At her sides are two suitor salkells that she's stopped kicking away. I caution Sanna against getting her hopes up that Meesahrah will settle with them, but the truth is, she's never shown this much attention to a pair of males before and I'm feeling rather hopeful myself.

The ship's main doors open, and the exit ramp thuds loudly to the ground.

Sanna heads for the ship, calling out a friendly, "Hi guys!"

Instead of hearing five Na'riths and Beth answer back—there's a thunder of paws and claws on shipdeck grating.

I reach Sanna just as Kota goes on the alert. "You may want to release her from work," I warn. "Otherwise she'll be sorely tested to complete her duty."

Spotting the miniscule versions of her kind, her tail wags wildly.

Loud yips and whimpers of excitement answer from the spacecraft gangplank—along with a ridiculous imitation of a commanding bark as the seven prick-eared tanks shiver with anticipation.

"Do you—" Sanna starts. "Do you hear that?"

"Oh, I hear it," I grin.

"That sounds like... Bres, are those *puppies?*"

Kota's last harness buckle drops just as she's met with a wall of madly barking, leaping alien creatures.

"Kota loves puppies," Sanna manages in a choked voice.

I hug her to my side. "So you said."

Meesahrah honks. Her ears are crossed and her dimpled chin is dropped in shock. Meanwhile, the rest of the Narwari are lined up, all focused stares as if the puppies are their next meal. We'll have to nip that misconception in the bud. "Let's get them in the round pen. The sides are high enough they won't get out, and it'll give them a chance to run around safely." I lead, Kota races around me in circles, and puppies give her chase. When we arrive at the soft-sand filled pen, Sanna reaches out to open the gate, and when the last pup makes it through, I let Sanna know it's safe to push the gate shut.

Twenty-eight stubby, thick-boned legs gallop after Kota who leaps on the flatbed and wags her tail madly as she stares down at all of her new friends/playmates from a safe distance.

With their prey out of their reach, they're stymied, and I'm chuckling until they turn as one for my female.

"Not a chance, you little ankle-munching aliens," I chastise, and I sweep Sanna up and into the safety of my arms. "Would you like to meet them one at a time, salk?" I ask her, thinking to set her on the flatbed with Kota and handing her pups one by one.

Her tear-dampened lashes sweep her cheeks as her face splits in a wide grin. "Nah, let me be covered in toothy puppies. But save me if I start to scream!" she laughs. "How many *are* there?" She kicks her feet happily. "They sound like shepherd puppies. Am I wrong?"

Before I answer, I devour her mouth.

Tiny pinprick teeth lock around my calf muscle. *It must be an alienbreed trait.* I let Sanna up for air, but nibble her lip as I answer. "You're not wrong. Prepare to meet the foundations of your very own kennel."

Sanna's hands catch me by my jaw spikes. "I love you so much."

I smile down at her radiant face. "Ready to love me more?"

"Is that even possible?"

She's talked so animatedly about her family's lines, I started committing ranch names—called kennel names for the species Earthens call *canines*—to memory. Then I supplied Ekan with what he needed to know in order to begin tracking them down.

I rattle off the kennels this juvenile stock hails from—and Sanna begins to cry. By the time I reach the name of her own family's kennel, the same one Kota is out of—Sanna is sobbing.

"Sanna," I say thickly as I raise her tighter to my chest in a bid to heartmeld her tears away. "My intention was not to break your heart."

"You didn't," she cries. "You just made it fall for you a little more."

"Ah, in that case, I'm glad to see that my plan worked," I mutter huskily. I want to kiss her again, but now I've collected *five* distinct sets of jaws clamped at various points on my legs, and the woman I love has professed an enthusiasm for catching these furred menace's interest. "I'm going to lower you as a puppy sacrifice now. Prepare yourself."

She's trying not to cry even as she's bursting with laughter. "I'm ready! *Drop me!*"

Shifting her to a—momentarily—puppy-free area, I do as my laughing female says: I open my arms and let her fall.

Is the dog okay?

^^THIS HAS BEEN *the number one question,* again and again, since Stolen by an Alien came out. Kota was only mentioned in Two Sentences, but the response was beautifully astounding. Amazon to Bookbub, the burning need to know about this guide dog's welfare has popped up in questions and comments as readers were driven to close their kindle covers and hunt for answers.

That. Is. COOL.

Thank you to everyone who reached out to me and offered to fact check a story lived through a blind woman. You guys are amazing! To author Shannon Gayle for dropping everything for this story and for saying yes to an interview. THANK YOU.

Loud cheers and free S'mores to my ARC Team for pulling double duty and being AWESOME. =D

Thank you to the amazing book blogs who help spread the word and share booklove: Nancy at East Coast Book Chicks & VanSpunky, Boundless Book Reviews, Veronica Scott's beautiful slice of Happy Ever After at USA Today, Nights of Passion Blog, Bubbles the Book Pimp, Psychotic Chipmunk's blog, Under the Covers Book Blog, After Dark Book Lovers blog, Lisa with Unlimited Book Reviews on Youtube, and more—you're *gems.*

To everyone who nominated Arokh, and voted for him in the Best Possessive Hero Awards, *awww!* *HEART EYES* YOU GUYS!!! *Thank You.*

Thank you to April and Megan for running the Book Recommendations group on Facebook like *bosses.* <3 Thank you to the

members of both groups for bringing great memes, funny clips, the
perfect GIFS to get through the day, and the most heartwarming well
wishes. *I LOVE YOU GUYS!!!*

And **thank YOU** for clicking this story: if you're new to alien
romance or if you're an alien-rom veteran with a fictional bookharem
of more alien boyfriends than you've got rooms in your house—I hope
you enjoyed the ride. :}

I know this book is a little different from the rest of the series and
readers are going to be wondering if you think this story is worth their
time. All of the unicorn-horn powder I was able to trade for has been
stuffed into these pages with the yearning that it'll hit you in the happy
feels and if you get the time to tap out a review to tell them so, *you have
my sincerest gratitude!* ♥

Thanks for reading Sanna and Breslin *and Kota's* story! :D

(...And Meesahrah's XD)

Much, much love,

Amanda

www.AmandaMilo.com[1]

Newsletter: https://bit.ly/2DlAKR7

*P.S. Read on for a cool Interview, Book Recommendations and Book
Links...*

---

1.   http://www.amandamilo.com

Interview with Shannon Gayle

WHEN PEOPLE LEARNED that I was writing this book, they had questions about those who experience the world different than they do. So when Author Shannon Gayle approached me with, *"I happen to be blind myself, and, if you ever do decide to write that story, I'd love to offer any help I can about getting blindness right,"* I did what anyone would do: I captured her to keep next to my writing desk (not *really*, but kind of) and asked if she'd be up for being interviewed too.

Spoiler alert: She said yes. :D

I've since had many, many wonderful individuals introduce themselves and offer help. It's been fascinating—everybody's experience is different, everybody's preferences are different. For example: some blind individuals are perfectly happy with their canes as their mobility aids and for various reasons choose *not* to have a guide dog.

To everyone that reached to me: THANK YOU.

Without further ado, let's hop into the interview.

Amanda: *Danke schön,* Shannon! Are ya Ready? =D

Amanda: Tell us about your job. Please =)

Shannon: I work for our state's library for the blind, so I know that the experience of a young person who is blind and an elderly person is different. I've never been able to see, so it's always been easier for me to adapt and find accommodations I need because I've always had to. Most of my elderly patrons don't have that frame of reference and a loss of vision is just one more way their body shuts down, you know?

Amanda: You're on Facebook! How do you read?

Shannon: I use a screen reader that renders text both on my computer and my phone.

Amanda: Can it read emojis?

Shannon: It handles emojis pretty well, so I can read them! Although I was using the old-fashioned emoticons all the time before that was a thing. :P

Amanda: That's so cool!! Can your reader read GIFs?

Shannon: Sadly, no gifs. I can make memes work sometimes because I can port the photo into another app that will read the text, but gifs don't render at all. So half the time I feel like I'm having the Facebook equivalent of conversations where I'm listening in to one half of a telephone call.

Amanda: Very good to know!

In the story, Sanna mentions she wears dark glasses to avoid being harassed when she takes Kota to certain establishments. Possibly due to portrayal in television shows and movies, there's a perception that if a person is blind, they automatically wear dark shades—but what's your experience?

Shannon: My personal experience is that I don't. But a lot of blind people find it easier to wear them, especially if they're sensitive to light. I'm not especially light-sensitive, and in fact I have pretty good light perception, so the shades would hinder me more than they'd help.

These were submitted questions:

I'm always spilling/feeding food to my shirt. How does a blind person clean up stains on their clothing?

Shannon: If I catch it, I always daub the area with cold water right away. Sometimes I have to get some help applying stain remover, but the real answer to this question is that I try really hard not to wear white if I can avoid it. And periodically I get people to help me go through my clothes and throw away anything that has obvious stains I didn't notice.

When you're walking around town or a city, how often do you get lost?

Shannon: I know the routes I take to work, and to some of the places I go to most frequently. When I don't, I try to take steps to mitigate that, like by getting clear directions beforehand or taking a taxi somewhere so I don't have to walk through several blocks of unfamiliar neighborhoods.

Do you have a guide dog?

Shannon: I do not. I'd like to, but at this point it's not practical. (I keep getting really close to applying to guide dog schools, and then my circumstances keep changing. At this point who knows if it'll ever happen?)

Do you read braille?

Shannon: I do! Also I'm very passionate about Braille literacy. These days for fun I mostly listen to books, but I do read Braille for my job. I don't have statistics, but I do know that 90 percent of the blind people I know who are employed are fluent Braille readers.

Amanda: *THANK YOU SO MUCH,* Shannon!! Is there anything you wished more people knew?

Shannon: Honestly, I wish people wouldn't be afraid [of being blind]. People have a perception that blindness has to be a state of complete dependence, but I live a fulfilling life on my own terms, the same way anyone else would.

About the Author

AMANDA MILO IS A COLLECTOR of the randomest trivia. *Did you know that Kiwi fruit plants have separate genders?* You need both in order to make Kiwi fruits happen. Isn't that cool?

She's concerned about river otter bite pressure—she hasn't had a chance to test this out, but frankly, this is the part that's holding her back from appropriating and testing the relocation (aka wildlife theft) of a small family of adorable river otters.

...To the bathtub. *(They're basically like slick-furred rubber duckies, but with lots of teeth, right? Right.)*

Extended contemplation of this plan has led to the permission to adopt more ferrets, which makes her very happy. So does her extensive, wacky-patterned, thigh-high sock collection—though ferrets, it must be noted, do not play well with pretty socks. *The crazy, clawed thieves!*

She invites you to hang out with her in the Amanda Milo's Minions Facebook group. (She didn't name the group! XD Readers have great senses of humor!)

If you haven't been sucked into Facebook yet, she's not quite as easy to capture—but when she has an internet connection, she'll do her best to reply at AmandaMiloBooks@gmail.com

Made in United States
Troutdale, OR
11/12/2024

24707981R00121